SLIME DOESN'T PAY!

SERIES BY R. L. STINE

GOOSEBUMPS

The Original Series
Series 2000
Give Yourself Goosebumps
Give Yourself Goosebumps: Special Edition
Goosebumps HorrorLand
Hall of Horrors
Goosebumps SlappyWorld

THE NIGHTMARE ROOM

The Original Series
The Nightmare Room Thrillogy

MOSTLY GHOSTLY

ROTTEN SCHOOL

FEAR STREET

R. L. STINE

SLIME
DOESN'T PAY!

**BLACK
STONE**
PUBLISHING

Printed in the United States of America

First edition: 2023
ISBN 979-8-212-51322-7
Juvenile Fiction / Horror

Version 1

Blackstone Publishing
31 Mistletoe Rd.
Ashland, OR 97520

www.BlackstonePublishing.com

To Dylan and Mia

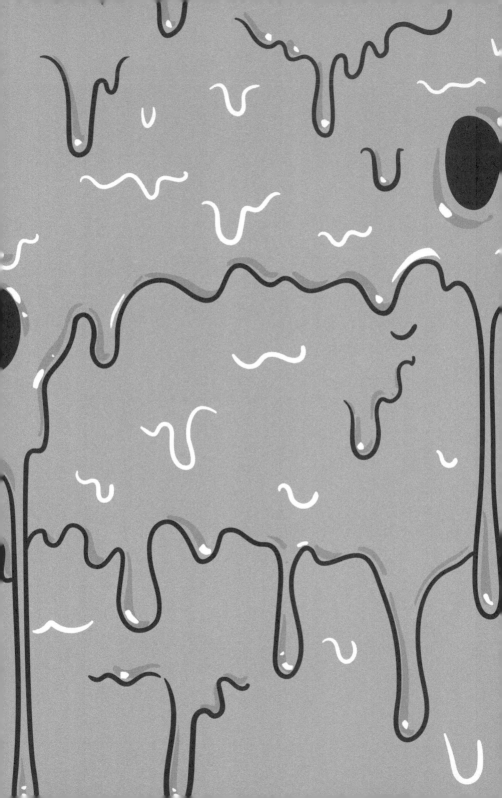

PROLOGUE

I did something horrible to my brother.

I'm not kidding.

I can't believe I did it.

If I explain it to you, maybe you'll understand why I did it. Or maybe you won't.

Once you hear my side of the story, you won't hate me. You'll agree with me. I hope you'll see that I had no choice.

My little brother, Arnie, has always been a pain.

I know, I know. All little brothers are a pain.

But Arnie was worse than a pain. He was a pain

and a headache. He was *ten* pains rolled into one little eight-year-old. But my parents never did anything about it. They said he'd outgrow it. But he was getting worse every day.

You've got to believe me. He was making my life impossible.

And then he did something horrible to me. Something unspeakable. Unforgivable.

And that's why I did what I did.

I admit it. What I did to Arnie wasn't right. What I did to Arnie changed our lives forever.

But listen to my side of the story. When you hear it, I know you'll understand.

Maybe, just maybe, you would have done the same terrible thing.

Where shall I start?

I guess I'll start at the sleepover I had with my friends one Friday night . . .

CHAPTER 1

SOMETHING HIDING IN THE CLOSET?

"Amy, please," Lissa said, rolling her eyes. "Please don't tell me you invited Marta to the sleepover tonight."

"Sorry. Marta is coming," I said. "I had to invite her."

"Had to?" Lissa made a spitting noise with her lips. "She's not even our friend, Amy."

"She *thinks* she is," I said. "And I couldn't leave her out. There's a reason."

Lissa took a long sip from the straw in her juice box. She has yellow-green eyes, and when she gets excited, they glow like headlights. It's kinda scary.

We were sitting cross-legged on the rug in my bedroom, our backs against my bed. "Marta ruins everything," Lissa said. "She talks about herself nonstop and how she's so smart and talented. And she brags about how her family goes to France every summer, and how she won that chess tournament when she was only five, and—"

"Tell me something I don't know," I said. My juice made a gurgling sound in the straw as I sucked up the last of it. I crushed the box in my hand and tossed it across the room to the wastebasket. Missed.

Lissa tore off the scrunchie holding her pony-tail and shook her head, letting her dark hair tumble down to her shoulders. "So what's the reason?"

I hesitated. Lissa and I have been best friends for three years, since third grade. We get along perfectly. We almost never argue about anything. But she has this habit of getting on my case because she says I'm too nice.

Too nice and too cooperative and I don't stand up for myself. I let other people tell me what to do.

That's what she accuses me of, and maybe she's right. But it's not like I'm unhappy all the time and feel like people push me around too much. I like being nice. It's not exactly a crime.

Lissa tugged at a strand in the shag rug. "So? The reason?"

"My mom made me invite Marta," I said. "Mom is trying to get a job with Marta's dad, and—"

"I get it," Lissa said. "So we have to be super nice to Marta."

"It's serious," I said. "Mom and Dad have been out of work for months. Mom says if they can't find jobs,

7

they'll have to sell this house and move to another town that's cheaper."

Lissa's eyes flashed wide again. "Oh no. That would be horrible."

I nodded. "Yeah. I know."

"How would you do my algebra homework for me?" Lissa said. "On FaceTime?"

"You're not funny," I muttered.

"I'd die if you moved away," she said. "I mean, literally."

"Then be nice to Marta," I replied.

She hopped up onto the bed. "Can we change the subject? Have you thought about Photo Day?"

I had to scoot around so I could face her. "Photo Day? It's coming up, right? Yeah. I've thought about it."

"Do you know what you're going to wear?"

"I'll show you," I said. I put my hands on her knees and used them to push myself to my feet. "Mom said we couldn't afford to buy anything new. But she found a real bargain at Stafford's."

"Where they have the used clothes?" She started to follow me to my closet.

"It's like new," I said. "You'll love it. It's a tunic dress with puffy sleeves."

"What color is it?"

"It's slate colored," I answered. "Very sophisticated."

The doorbell chimed. I stopped with my hand on the closet doorknob. "That's probably Sophie," I said. "She always comes early."

"I'll get it." Lissa turned and ran out into the hall.

The doorbell chimed again.

"I'm coming!" she shouted. The sound of her running footsteps faded as she headed to the front door.

I started to pull open my closet. But I stopped when I heard a sound. A low growl. Like an angry dog.

Inside the closet?

I froze with my hand gripping the doorknob. "Arnie? Is that you?" I demanded.

My little brother is a beast. No joke. It wouldn't be the first time he hid in my closet and spied on Lissa and me.

"Arnie?"

A harsh animal snarl was the reply. Then scraping

sounds. Like fingernails scratching the inside of the closet door.

"Arnie—come out of there. You're not funny."

I twisted the knob, swung open the door—and screamed in shock as something leaped out at me.

A black blur. A hissing blur.

It flew up from the closet floor and bumped my shoulders, hit me hard, pushing me back. I groaned and fell backward. "Owwww!" I cried out as my head bounced on the floor.

Spitting and hissing, the creature landed on top of me. I saw red eyes. Black fur. Spiky quills like a porcupine. Long, curled yellow teeth slick with drool.

"Help me! Help me! Lissa! Mom! Dad! Help!"

SLIME DOESN'T PAY!

CHAPTER 2

IS ARNIE OKAY?

The creature opened its jaws wide, its red eyes glaring into mine. Hot, sticky drool dripped onto my face.

"*Help*—somebody!"

Without thinking, I shot up both hands and shoved the beast off me.

It groaned and snapped its curled teeth. Its drool splattered the rug this time. The long talons on its front paws got tangled in my hair. With a grunt, it tugged itself free. Growling, it darted out of the room, black quills quivering behind it.

A putrid odor floated over me. The creature smelled like rotten fish.

I held my breath to keep the smell out. Shaking, I forced myself to my feet.

I stared into the open closet.

What was that awful creature? How did a wild animal get into the house? How did it get in my closet?

Wiping the sticky drool off my face with the sleeve of my shirt, I ran into the hall. "Did you see it?" I cried. "Did you? Did you see that . . . thing?"

Lissa spun away from the front door. My friends Sophie and Marta had stepped into the house. They were pulling off their coats.

"See what?" Lissa asked. She saw the alarm on my face. "Amy, what's wrong?"

"Didn't you see it?" I shouted. "It was bigger than Aunt Helen's dog. It . . . it ran out into the hall. You *had* to see it! It was . . . a monster!"

Marta laughed. "You mean Arnie?"

Sophie let out a scream. "An animal in the house?" she cried. "Where? Where is it?" She shoved her back against the wall and raised her coat in front of her to protect herself.

Sophie isn't exactly the bravest person I know.

Marta squinted at me, trying to decide if she believed me or not.

"Didn't you see it?" I cried. "It . . . jumped out of the closet. It . . . it was covered in quills. It had red eyes, and it drooled on me."

"Yuck!" Marta and Sophie both exclaimed. Sophie huddled next to Marta.

"I didn't see anything," Lissa said. "It didn't come this way."

"That means it's still in the house!" Sophie cried.

We froze for a moment. Listening. I gazed up and down the hall.

"You're sure it wasn't Arnie?" Marta said. She tossed her coat onto the floor. She never hangs it up.

"You *had* to see it!" I screamed. "It was an animal! A *creature*!"

"Oh, I get it," Sophie said. "We're doing another Fright Night." She shivered. "Do we have to? After that last scary movie, I had nightmares for a week."

I shook my fists in front of me. "Why don't you believe me?" I cried. "We're not doing Fright Night. It was terrifying. It—it—"

Mom stepped into the front hall. She had just gotten out of the shower. Her blond hair was wrapped in a towel, but a few strands had escaped and dripped water onto the shoulders of her sweatshirt.

"What's all the shouting about?" she demanded.

"Amy saw an animal in her closet," Marta said. She snickered.

Mom turned to me. "You saw *what*?"

"S-Some kind of creature," I stammered. "It was big and heavy. It knocked me over. It had long, spiky quills on its back and—"

"A porcupine?" Mom said, gazing down the hall. "In your room?"

"I don't think it was a porcupine," I said. "It was too big. It hissed at me and—"

"Remember when that raccoon got in the garage?" Mom said. She doesn't like any kind of trouble. She always changes the subject immediately.

"Martinvale Woods is only two blocks away,"

Lissa said. "Lots of animals come out of the woods. I think—"

"I think you should call Animal Control," Sophie said, still shielding herself with her coat. "They'll send someone to capture it." She swallowed. "Maybe we should cancel the sleepover."

"No way!" Lissa cried. "We don't even know if the animal is still in the house."

"Let's search for it," I said.

Marta nodded. "This is such a small house. It won't take long."

Marta lives in a big house on the other side of Martinvale Woods. It has three floors, an attic, a big roof terrace, and a four-car garage. I'm sure she feels cramped in our little ranch-style house, all on one floor.

But she didn't have to *say* it.

Typical Marta.

Mom rubbed her hands together. "Let's split up and search the house," she said.

"Can't we do it together?" Sophie asked.

"Okay. Together," I said. I turned and started walking along the hall toward the back of the house.

"I was in my bathroom brushing my hair," Mom said, following close behind me. "It didn't come anywhere near there."

"Where's Dad?" I asked, suddenly remembering he was missing.

"Believe it or not, he has a late job interview," Mom replied. "It's the only time the guy could see him. He's two towns away in Marion Mills."

We stayed close together as we walked. We peeked into the kitchen. Lissa pulled up the tablecloth and peered under the kitchen table. No creature.

No sign of it in the living room or the den or Dad's small home office. My parents' room was next. Then my room.

Where is it? I asked myself. *If it didn't run out the door, it has to be in the house!*

"We're almost out of rooms," Marta said. "You don't have a basement, right?"

Arnie's room stood at the end of the hall. The door was closed.

I raised my fist and pounded on the door. "Arnie?"

"Arnie? Are you in there?" Lissa called.

We gazed at each other, waiting for him to answer.

"I think he said he had homework to do," Mom said.

I laughed. "Mom, when have you ever seen Arnie do homework?"

I pounded on the door again. "Arnie—open up!" I shouted.

I put my ear to the door. I didn't hear him moving to let us in.

"Arnie! Hey—Arnie! Open the door!" Lissa called.

Silence.

Not a sound from the other side of the door.

A wave of fear rolled down my back. I turned to Mom. "Why doesn't he answer? Is he okay?"

CHAPTER 3

QUILLS

Sophie squeezed my shoulder. "Maybe the animal ran in there? Do you think it's in there with Arnie?"

"I don't know," I said. "It's possible. If his door was open . . ."

Sophie gasped. "Oh no. The poor kid. We have to call 911. We have to call—"

Arnie's door swung open. He gazed out at us with a surprised expression on his face. I saw a set of VR goggles in his hand.

"What's your problem?" he asked.

"Why didn't you answer?" I cried.

"Cuz I knew it was you," he said.

So nasty. Arnie looks like an angel with his curly blond hair and blue eyes and freckles around his nose. But he'd have to change his whole personality for anyone to think he was one.

"What were you doing in there?" Mom demanded. She pushed the door open farther and peered into his room.

Arnie raised the goggles. "I was doing some VR stuff. Actually, I was fighting alien invaders on the moon. How was I supposed to hear you from the moon?"

"Alien invaders? What happened to your home-work?" Mom asked.

He shrugged. "Beats me. Guess I didn't get to it."

"Never mind that," I said. "Did you see anything strange?"

Arnie smiled. "You mean, besides you?" He laughed at his own joke. He thinks he's a riot.

Marta frowned at him. "How old are you, Arnie?"

"Eight," he answered. "Same as your IQ!"

Isn't he the worst?

"Okay, girls, let's leave the comedian alone," Mom said. She pulled Lissa and me back from the doorway. "Arnie, I made my homemade pizza, and I put extra salami and hot dogs on it. Would you like to join the girls and have a slice?"

Arnie thought about it for a few seconds. "Join the girls? Could I cut off my head instead?" He closed his bedroom door.

Marta made a disgusted face. "Is your brother always like this?"

"He usually isn't that nice," I said.

Everyone laughed.

I led the way to the kitchen. The aroma of Mom's home-baked pizza floated into the hall. She bakes a pizza every Friday night, and it's the *best*.

Usually, just thinking about it puts me in a good mood. But tonight I couldn't shake off my troubled feelings. How could that big animal disappear into thin air?

It didn't run out the front door. Lissa, Marta, or Sophie would have seen it. We had searched every room from one end of the hallway to the other. And it was chilly out, so all the windows were closed.

I have a very good imagination. Everyone tells me that. I like to write fantasy stories and create all kinds of weird plots and characters. Sometimes my mind drifts just thinking about new stories.

But I didn't make up the big creature that knocked me over in my room. No way. It was very real.

Lissa put an arm around my shoulders as we walked. "Amy, are you okay? Where do you think the creature went?" she asked.

"Daydream much?" Marta said from behind us.

"It wasn't a dream," I snapped. "It knocked me over."

"Can we please stop talking about it?" Sophie said.

We stepped into the kitchen and were hit by a blast of hot air.

Mom let out a cry. "Hey—the oven! Why is the oven door open?"

She ran to the stove, and we followed. The oven door was down. Inside, the pizza had been pulled half-way off its pan. Cheese had melted onto the metal rack and dripped to the floor of the oven.

"Who was in here? How did this happen?" Mom cried.

I grabbed an oven mitt off the counter. Then I squatted onto my knees, reached into the oven, and started to slide the melting pizza back onto its pan.

"Whoa." I stopped and jerked my gloved hand out. I leaned into the heat and squinted hard at the top of the pizza.

"Amy? What's wrong?" Mom asked, leaning over me.

"Something on top of the pizza," I murmured. "Something . . ."

I reached into the oven again. Waves of heat roared out at me. Squinting against them, I plucked something off the pizza.

A thick strand of cheese stuck to the oven mitt. I pulled my arm out and climbed to my feet. Stepping away from the oven, I stared down at the mitt.

Mom stared over my shoulder. "What is it?" she asked.

"Quills," I said. "Black quills."

CHAPTER 4

THE MONSTER IS BACK

Sophie slapped her hands over her mouth. "I . . . I'm going to be sick," she said.

Lissa led her away from the oven.

"What kind of animal breaks into an oven to get pizza?" Marta said, gazing at the quills in the oven mitt.

"A clever one," Lissa said. "That oven isn't easy to open."

Marta made a disgusted face. "Yuck. We don't have to eat that—do we?"

"Is the creature still in the oven?" Sophie called, her hands covering her face.

Mom pulled on her oven mitts, removed the ruined pizza from the oven, and carried it to the sink. "No," she told Sophie. "The animal isn't in there."

She heaved the pizza into the trash. "I'll call for pizza delivery. It won't take long."

The kitchen window rattled in a strong gust of wind. Outside, I could see the backyard trees shaking against the gray evening sky.

I realized I still held the long black quills. I pulled them off the oven mitt and tossed them into the trash. Then I took off the mitt and washed my hands in the kitchen sink.

"What if that animal is still in the house?" Sophie said. "What if it's hiding somewhere?"

"Do you want to search again?" I asked her. "We looked very carefully."

Mom was on the phone with the Pizza Pit, a few minutes away.

I heard thumping noises in the hallway.

Sophie gasped. "What *is* that?"

Arnie walked into the room. "It's me," he said. He

sniffed the air. "Mmmm. Smells good. Did you save me a slice?"

I laughed and opened the door to the cabinet with the trash can. "You can have the whole thing," I told him. "Go ahead. Dig in."

He scrunched his face up, puzzled, and peered into the trash. "What happened?" he asked Mom. "You burned it? Again?"

"I never burned it before," Mom replied. "Amy likes it well done."

"The pizza got infested," Marta told him.

Arnie looked like he wanted to hurl one of his nasty insults at her. But for once, he didn't. "Weird," he muttered instead.

"I ordered pizzas from the Pizza Pit," Mom told him.

He narrowed his blue eyes at her. "Did you remember to order extra pepperoni? They never put on enough."

"No, I didn't," Mom said. "But I think you'll survive."

"This is *my* slumber party," I told him. "It isn't about you."

He reached into the trash can and pulled up a

gloppy hunk of pizza. "Hungry? Eat some. *Eat* it!" He smashed it into my face.

"Ohhhh, yuck!" The hot cheese stung my cheeks and went up my nose. I screamed and started to tug it off with both hands.

"Arnie!" Mom yelled at him.

He laughed, spun around, and went running from the kitchen.

"How did he get to be such a brat?" Marta asked.

"Practice," I said.

I heard Arnie's footsteps thudding down the hall. And then . . . a hard bump, and he let out a sharp cry.

Did he fall?

"Amy, I tripped over it!" he screeched. "That creature! It's back!"

CHAPTER 5

BEFORE THE REAL HORROR BEGINS

Sophie gasped and stumbled back against the kitchen table.

I froze for a moment and made a choking sound. Lissa and I exchanged glances. We pushed past Marta and my mom, bumping each other as we bolted into the hall.

My eyes squinted into the bright hall light, searching for the creature. Arnie stood near the den, leaning against the wall.

"Where is it?" I screamed. "Where?"

A grin slowly spread over his face as Lissa and I skidded to a stop.

He snickered. "Just messing with you."

"Huh?" I gasped. "You mean—?"

Arnie laughed. "Messing with you," he repeated.

I swung both hands up and tried to grab him by the neck so I could strangle him. But he was too fast. He ducked and took off running to his room at the end of the hall.

Lissa and I started after him, but we stopped after a few steps. What was the point?

He was still laughing as he slammed his bedroom door shut.

Lissa shook her head. "Your brother is about as funny as a toothache," she said. Lissa had a toothache last year, which must have been pretty bad. Because she still talks about it.

"*He* thinks he's funny," I said. "He doesn't care what we think."

The others were waiting for us outside the kitchen.

"Did you see it? Where was it?" Sophie demanded.

Lissa rolled her eyes. "The only creature we saw was Arnie."

"He was playing a stupid joke," I said.

"Glad I don't have a brother," Marta said. She shuddered. "I don't even like to think about it."

Marta loves being an only child. She even brags about how much attention she gets and how she doesn't have to share Christmas presents.

At her house, there's an extra bedroom next to hers. And she uses that one, too. She actually has *two* bedrooms!

I have to share my room with Mom's sewing machine. It's my bedroom *and* her sewing room.

Arnie's room used to be a walk-in closet. Marta has no idea how lucky she is.

"Come on, let's go to your room. I brought new nail polish colors!" Lissa said.

My mom went to clean out the oven as we made our way down the hall. But I had a hard time focusing on choosing a color. My stomach was rumbling, for one thing, and my gaze kept wandering to my closet door.

Thankfully, the doorbell rang a few minutes later. It was the pizza delivery guy.

Lissa and I carried the two boxes into the kitchen.

Sophie held her hand on her stomach. "I don't know if I can ever eat pizza again," she said. "I keep seeing those awful black quills stuck in the cheese, and I want to puke."

I pulled up the box lid. "No quills on this one," I said. "You should give it a try."

I started to tug out slices and put them on plates.

"Should we call Arnie in?" Mom asked.

"Let's wait till the pizza gets cold, then let him in," Marta said.

We all laughed.

Sometimes I admire Marta's dry sense of humor, especially when she's talking about my brother. She's a spoiled brat, but she can be very funny.

The four of us sat around the kitchen table and ate pizza. We tried to have a normal conversation. Marta wanted to talk about Photo Day. And Lissa and I wanted to talk about our parts in the school musical.

The drama club was doing *Fiddler on the Roof* next month. Lissa and I played two of Tevye's daughters—he's the star of the show—and Lissa even had a song to perform.

But we were quieter than usual. We usually tease each other, and talk about some of the boys in our class, and gossip about our teachers, and laugh a lot.

But I kept listening for sounds in the hallway. I was listening for footsteps, animal footsteps. Sophie ate only half a slice and kept glancing at the kitchen doorway.

And as hard as we tried not to mention it again, I know the messed-up pizza with the disgusting quills in the open oven was still on everyone's mind.

How could we not think about it?

We all gasped when the kitchen door swung open. But it was only Dad, back from his job interview.

He waved hello to everyone and pulled off his coat. "Did you save me a slice?" he asked. He looked tired.

"There's plenty," Mom said. She jumped up from the table and walked over to him. "How was the job interview?"

He shook his head. "Sid said the TV people aren't hiring production help. He knows I know my way around a studio. I even offered to be a prop guy. But, no luck."

"Something will turn up." Mom patted his

shoulder. "Anyway, we've had some excitement here," she told him.

He squinted at her. "Excitement?"

"A vicious animal running through the house."

"Oh. The usual," he said. He grabbed a pizza slice from the box and raised it to his mouth.

"Let's talk about it later," I said. I could see how bad Dad looked. His shoulders were hunched over. And he had dark circles under his eyes.

Why trouble him with it now?

He turned to everyone at the table. "You can't have a slumber party without a vicious animal loose in the house," he said.

Everyone but Sophie laughed at that.

"You've seen too many horror movies," I told him.

We finished the pizza, grabbed bottles of water and bags of chips, and hurried to my room. I pulled the window blind down as we changed into our nightshirts and pajamas.

My room faces the front of the house, and our house is very close to the street. Anyone walking by on the sidewalk can see inside easily.

A sliver of a yellow moon still hung low in the night sky. The streetlight flashed on at the curb just as I pulled down the blind.

It's always hot in my room, so I leave the window open. A gentle breeze ruffled the blind.

"Amy, are you sure those pj's are big enough?" Marta asked. "Did you get them at a clown costume store?"

"Give me a break. I like them baggy," I said. I

admired her outfit, silky maroon shorts and a buttoned top. "Are those real silk?"

"I didn't really check," she replied. "Probably."

"Don't you slide right out of bed?" Lissa asked her.

Marta stared at Lissa but didn't reply.

We settled on my bed and the couch next to it to watch some YouTube videos. And we had our usual slumber party argument. Sophie and Marta wanted to watch music videos. Lissa and I wanted to watch this awesome do-it-yourself channel called The Unwatchables. In the videos, these teenagers make incredibly impossible contraptions and then wreck them.

We were getting comfortable. We were finally starting to relax and enjoy ourselves.

We didn't know we were moments away from when the *real* horror would begin.

CHAPTER 6

THE BURGLAR
SPOILS THE PARTY

First, we danced to some music videos. The kind of wild, crazy dancing you do when no one is watching. Sophie is timid and shy, but she's a very good dancer. She takes a ballet class after school twice a week. It was great to see her loosen up a bit.

Then we switched to The Unwatchables. Lissa and I really love it. The teenagers on the show have millions of followers. In this video, they were smashing pineapples with a hammer so they could build a birdhouse out of fruit.

Marta sat on the couch next to Sophie. Lissa and I were sprawled on my bed.

"Are you ready for Photo Day?" Marta asked me.

I shrugged. "I'm not sure. I have a new dress—"

"You should wear that clown suit," she said. "That would look awesome in the yearbook."

I tugged the pajama pants up. "It's not a clown suit," I muttered. "Let me show you the dress I got."

I hopped off the bed and crossed the room to the closet. I gripped the door handle, then stopped.

I had forgotten about the big creature for a few minutes. Now it all came back to me.

Was it hiding in there? Was that why we couldn't find it? Did it run back into the closet? Was it preparing to leap out at me again?

"Amy, what's wrong?" Lissa called.

"Nothing," I said. I took a deep breath. Then I turned the knob and pulled open the closet door.

Empty.

No creature greeted me. I clicked on the closet

light, found the new dress, and pulled it out. "What do you think?"

"Wow. I don't believe it," Marta said. "That's my old dress. From fourth grade. I sold it to the second-hand store! Is that where you got it?"

Everyone grew silent. I could feel my face turn hot and knew I was blushing.

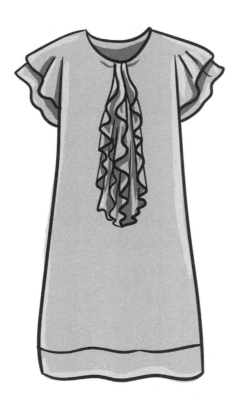

It was seriously embarrassing. What were the chances of me buying Marta's old dress?

I decided to just carry on. Pretend I hadn't heard her.

I held it up in front of me. "I have these maroon tights to wear under it," I said.

"Love the frilly ruffle going down the front," Sophie said.

"I don't think of you as frilly," Marta said to me. "But I always liked that dress. I wore it a lot. Don't you remember?"

I ignored her question. "What are *you* going to wear?" I asked Marta.

She shrugged. "I haven't thought about it. I never get dressed up for Photo Day. I mean, whatever."

"I can't find a good baby picture I like," Sophie said.

We were supposed to bring in baby pictures on Photo Day. They would go side by side with our new photos in the yearbook.

"I was bald till I was three," Sophie said. "So my baby pictures are gross."

"You'd look adorable bald," Marta told her. "Like a melon on legs."

43

The video on the laptop caught my eye. "What are the Unwatchables making?" I asked.

Everyone turned to the screen. The two guys and a girl had a big plastic container, the size of a kitchen trash can, on a table. One of the guys filled it halfway with water. Then the other guy tilted a gallon bottle of detergent into the container. Next, the girl tossed in handfuls of flour.

A caption came on the screen. It read:

"This is the only recipe for blue slime you'll ever need," the girl said into the camera. *"For the complete recipe, click the link below."*

They added blue food coloring and more

ingredients. Then they stirred the whole thing with a long wooden spoon.

Another caption flashed on the screen:

"Who shall we slime today?" one guy asked, rubbing his hands together and making a devilish face.

"Here comes your cousin," the other guy said. *"Perfect timing."*

A short, skinny kid with spiky red hair, wearing a "Star Trek Forever" T-shirt over black jeans, wandered onto the screen. Before he could say a word, the girl and two guys hoisted the container over his head—and sent the blue slime splashing down over him.

He made a gurgling sound as he disappeared inside the blue wave. The slime was thick and sticky and oozed slowly down his body.

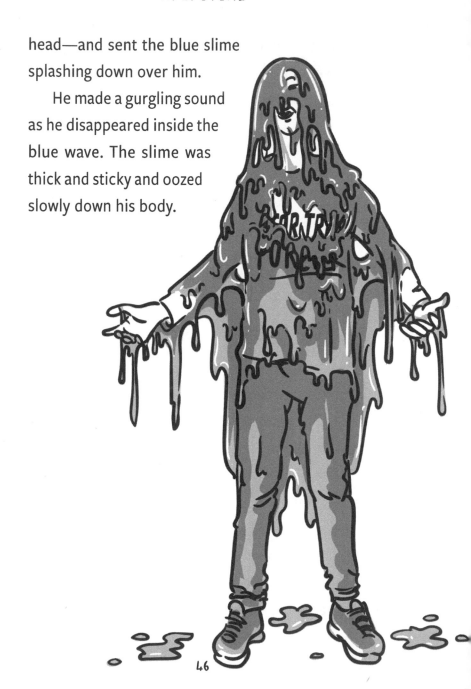

46

He thrashed his arms and tried to free himself. He grabbed at his face and struggled to pull the thick blanket of glop away so he could breathe.

The three slime makers watched, roaring with laughter, slapping each other high fives, falling to their knees in triumph.

Their victim staggered around the room and slipped on a puddle of slime. He made a loud *splosssh* sound as he hit the floor and flopped there like a fish. This made the other three laugh even harder.

"Looks like fun," Marta said. "We should make a batch of that stuff."

"And who would we dump it on?" I asked.

"Your brother, of course," Lissa said.

I laughed. I tried to picture it. Yes. Sliming Arnie would be fun.

I was still thinking about it when a sharp noise at the window made us all jump. I turned and saw that the window blind had snapped up.

I saw the streetlight out the window. The sliver of a moon had risen higher in the night sky.

I started to climb off the bed. "Maybe we should close the window. I think—"

I stopped with a gasp when I saw the black-gloved hand. The glove gripped the window ledge from outside. A second glove appeared.

I froze. It took me a few seconds to realize what was happening. I saw the front of a black sweater. And then an arm. And then a head appeared, completely covered in a black ski mask.

I opened my mouth and choked out a scream. "Help! Heeeeeeelp! A man is breaking in!"

CHAPTER 7

THE BURGLAR HOWLS

The gloved hands scrambled over the window ledge. The masked head poked into the room. I could hear the scraping sounds the man's shoes made against the brick wall outside as he struggled to force himself through the window.

"Mom! Dad! Help!" I screamed.

The four of us crashed into each other as we raced through the bedroom doorway. Lissa's elbow dug into my waist as she pushed herself past me.

We all ran screaming down the hall in our nightshirts and pajamas.

Where are my parents? Can't they hear our screams?

Lissa tore open the front door and ran out, leaping off the stoop into the yard. I followed close behind. "Whoa!" The grass was cold and wet from the evening dew.

I heard a scream—and spun around to see Marta on her stomach on the stoop. "Marta—!" I called to her. "Did you fall?"

"My knee!" she cried. "Owwww. I think . . . I think I broke it!"

Sophie had run to the driveway. Gravel stuck to her bare feet as she bolted to the street. Lissa and I trotted up the lawn to Marta. I reached down and helped her up. "Can you stand? Does your knee really hurt?"

She took a few hobbling steps, groaning with each one. "If my knee is broken, my parents will have to sue you," she muttered. "Look. Look. It's . . . bleeding!"

My mom and dad finally appeared in the doorway. "What's going on?" Dad cried. "Why are you girls out here in your pajamas? Did you move the party outside?"

"Dad—" I started. "A burglar. In the house."

"Didn't you hear us screaming?" Lissa cried.

"Our TV was too loud," Dad said. "We didn't hear anything."

"Call 911!" Sophie yelled from the street.

Mom and Dad exchanged glances. "A burglar? Where? In your room, Amy?" Mom said.

And then I saw the masked figure, dressed entirely in black, sneak up behind Mom and Dad.

"He—he's *right behind you!*" I screeched.

They both spun around and let out startled cries.

The burglar stepped quickly between them. He elbowed them roughly to the sides of the doorway.

"Don't hurt them!" I cried. "What do you want? What do you *want*?"

He didn't reply. He stood there staring out at us. The light from behind him in the hallway glowed around his black outfit. It made him look as if he was on fire.

I gasped as he reached up with both hands—and yanked the black wool ski mask off his face.

"You?" I cried. "It's YOU?!"

He tossed the mask at me, raised his face, and sent a howling laugh to the sky.

CHAPTER 8

GONE WITH THE WIND

I stared angrily at my cousin Max.

"Max! You scared us to death!" I shouted. "What are you doing here? Why—?"

My parents spun around to see him. "Max—did you deliberately scare the girls?" Mom demanded.

He finally stopped laughing. "It wasn't my idea," he replied. "But it sure worked. Look at them—still shaking!"

My cousin is eighteen, and he's big and wide. He's a tackle for the football team at the junior college.

Max looks menacing when he *isn't* wearing a mask and climbing into your window.

I curled my hands into angry fists and strode toward the house. "Max, why did you do it?" I demanded.

He grinned at me. "It wasn't my idea, Amy. It was Arnie's."

Arnie leaped out from behind him. He punched his hands in the air. "Victory! Victory!" he cried.

"Arnie called me," Max said. "He said your slumber party was too boring. No one was having a good time. He said you needed me to pick things up!"

I stepped up to Max and started punching him in the chest. He's almost two feet taller than me. He just laughed, grabbed my hands, and pushed me away.

I glared at my brother. "I should have known it was your idea."

"Because I'm a genius?" Arnie said.

"My knee really hurts," Marta said. "I'm calling my dad to come pick me up."

"I—I'm going home, too," Sophie stammered.

"That was the scariest moment of my life. I don't think I want to come to any more sleepovers."

I turned to my parents. "You have to do something. Don't you see? Arnie is ruining my life," I said.

"He's quite a joker," Dad said.

"Joker? JOKER?" I cried. I felt about to explode. Why didn't they ever *do* something about him?

"Is there any pizza left over?" Max asked. "Arnie said there was pizza. That's why I agreed to scare you. I'm totally starving."

"Your brother is a monster," Lissa said.

I rolled my eyes. "Tell me something I don't know."

She slid her hood up over her head, but the wind kept blowing it back. It made her hair fly around her head as if it were alive.

It was Tuesday after school, and we were still talking about Arnie's burglar trick. Lissa and I were walking to my house to rehearse our parts in the musical.

The sky was gray with storm clouds low overhead. We leaned forward as we walked, pushing against the wind's strong blasts.

"Marta's knee was really hurt Friday night," Lissa said, shouting over the gusts. "She said it took her parents forever to stop the bleeding."

I sighed. "And Arnie wouldn't even apologize. He was so proud of his burglar joke."

"It wasn't funny. It was sick," Lissa said. "Did you see Marta limping around school today?"

"She really was making the most of it," I said. "It was only a little swollen . . ."

"Lots of little brothers are pests," Lissa interrupted me. "That's their job. But Arnie . . ."

A truck rumbled past us on Chapel Street, and I didn't hear the rest of what she said.

"Arnie is a disaster," I said as we crossed the street. Cold raindrops started to drizzle down. "He loves making my life miserable. Even my parents don't know what to do with him."

Lissa shivered. Her hood blew off again. "And what is your cousin's problem?"

"He thinks Arnie is a riot," I said. "But he isn't funny. He's only mean."

My house came into view at the end of the block. We started to run.

As we reached the driveway, I was surprised to see Dad pull up in our car. Lissa and I stepped under the roof over the front stoop. We watched as Dad climbed out, followed by Arnie.

Dad waved as he trotted up to us. He looked even more weary than last week. His hair stuck out as if he'd forgotten to brush it. Arnie had the usual smirk on his face.

"Dad, what's up?" I asked.

He shrugged and pushed open the front door. "I had to pick Arnie up at school. He got into a little trouble."

A gust of wind followed us into the house. I closed the door behind us, and we all started to pull off our wet coats.

"No biggie," Arnie said. He heaved his coat at me.

"Yes, it was," Dad said sharply. "He cut off a girl's ponytail."

Lissa and I gasped.

"It was an accident," Arnie said. His smile stayed on his face.

"An accident? How could it be an accident?" I asked him.

"The scissors slipped." He giggled.

"Don't laugh!" Dad snapped. "It isn't funny. It's serious. We're going to have a family meeting about it after dinner."

"Do I have to come?" Arnie asked.

My parents would never dream of hitting one of us. But I sure felt like punching Arnie in the face. It wasn't the first time I'd had that feeling.

I realized my fists were clenched tightly at my sides. I let out a long breath and loosened them.

Lissa and I grabbed water bottles and a bag of oatmeal raisin cookies in the kitchen. Then I pulled the *Fiddler on the Roof* script from my backpack, and we went down the hall to my room.

I placed the script on the table by the window. We sat across from each other on the rug and had a few cookies to get carbed up and ready to rehearse.

Outside, the wind howled and rain pattered against the window. Arnie was in his room at the end of the hall, blasting hip-hop music as loud as he could. I climbed up and closed my bedroom door.

"I think we should start with your big scene," I told Lissa. "You're terrified because you have to tell Tevye, our father, that you want to get married and move away."

"Okay. Let's read through it," Lissa replied. "I don't really know it yet."

The script was long. I pulled the whole stack from the folder and carried it to the center of the room.

Then Lissa and I pawed through it, trying to find the scene.

"I'll play Tevye," I said. I pointed to the page. "Let's start here."

Lissa stepped close beside me so we could both see the script pages. "We should do the song, too," Lissa said. She shook her head. "Amy, you know I can barely carry a tune? How did I even get this part?"

"You'll be great," I said. "We'll rehearse it till you sound almost good."

That made her laugh.

Lissa is smart and good at just about everything she tries. But sometimes she has to be pushed a little.

I held the pages between us, and we started to read through the scene. Lissa was supposed to sound nervous. She knew our father would be shocked and maybe even angry about her news. But Lissa was trying too hard, and her voice kept cracking.

It made us both laugh. After a few more tries, we had to take a cookie-and-water break because we were both laughing too hard.

We started again, and it went much better.

Then we sang the song together a few times, and it didn't sound bad at all.

"Let's try it without the script," Lissa said. "See how we do."

She took the script from me and placed it back on the table by the window. Then she came back to the center of the room. "I think I know it all by heart," she said. "Let's see."

Before we could start the scene, the door opened. Arnie stepped into the room.

"Don't you ever knock?" I snapped.

"I don't think so," he said.

"Well, go away. Lissa and I are rehearsing."

"Can I watch?" he asked, walking up to us. "I'll be the audience."

"We don't want an audience," I said. "We need to practice without an audience."

"You're not nice," he said.

Lissa and I both laughed. "*WE* aren't nice?" we said together.

"Are you a little confused?" Lissa asked.

"Please go," I said. "I'm asking you nicely."

He crossed to the window.

"What are you doing?" I asked.

"It's too hot in here," he said. He started to lift the window.

"No—don't!" I cried. "It's too windy outside. The script will blow—"

He raised the window an inch.

"Arnie—don't!" I screamed. "Do you hear me? Don't!"

"Don't do it!" Lissa cried.

He pulled it open all the way.

A swirl of wind lifted the script pages up from the table. "Noooo!" The pages started to fly out the window, five or six at a time.

Lissa and I both jumped to our feet and dove for them. Too late. The strong gusts sucked the script into the yard.

"Ooops!" Arnie exclaimed. I reached out both hands to tackle him. But he danced away. "Oops. Ooops."

I stuck my head out the window, and the rain drenched my hair. I stared down at the script pages, blown all over the grass, soaked by the driving downpour.

Raindrops ran down my forehead. I turned to Arnie. "How could you?" I screamed. "How *could* you?"

"It was an accident," he said.

CHAPTER 9

THE MISSING BABY PICTURES

"Arnie, take the AirPods out of your ears," Dad said. "We're having a family meeting."

Arnie tugged the little white pods from his ears and burped really loud. "Good dinner, Mom."

Our dirty dishes were still on the table. Mom and Dad knew if we got up and carried them to the kitchen, Arnie would disappear into his room.

I took a sip of my iced tea and gazed across the table at him. *How can someone who looks so cute be so awful?* I asked myself.

And then another question ran through my mind: *Was Arnie ever nice?*

I pictured him as a baby, red-faced, wailing and crying all night. No one in the house ever got any sleep.

I pictured Grandma Beth when she came to visit. She leaned over Arnie's crib to say good night to him. And he bit her nose so hard she had to have stitches.

That was the last time she ever visited.

I remembered Mom and Dad had to meet with his first-grade teacher. Arnie was jumping on the other kids' shoulders and forcing them to take him for rides. Of course, the poor kids just collapsed beneath him.

This year, they had to meet with his third-grade teacher because he was stealing kids' lunch bags and stomping on them, crushing their lunches. He said he was practicing his tap dancing lessons.

She actually separated him from the rest of the class. She made him sit in a corner against the back wall by himself. She explained to my parents that Arnie hadn't done anything else bad. But she was sure that he soon would.

The kid has a bad reputation.

And now he sat at the dining room table, spinning the AirPods in his hands and tapping a foot on the floor, like he couldn't wait to leave.

"You need to take this seriously," Mom told him. "Cutting off a girl's hair is an attack. If her parents wanted to go to the police, you could end up in juvenile prison. Seriously."

"Juvenile prison?" Arnie said. "Cool. Do they have family meetings in juvenile prison?"

Dad hit the table with his fist, so hard the plates bounced. "You think you're being funny, but you're not."

Mom squeezed the napkin in her hand. "What can we do to make you change your attitude?" she asked.

"Well . . ." Arnie thought for a moment. "Do you have any cookie-dough ice cream? That might work."

"He's a jerk," I muttered.

"Amy, don't call your brother names," Dad said. "Arnie has some problems to work out and—"

"I don't have any problems," Arnie said. "Just you. You don't understand me."

"*We* don't understand *you*?" Mom cried. "What don't we understand?"

"I like to have fun," he replied. "You don't understand about having fun."

Mom and Dad just stared back at him. Dad

opened his mouth to say something but changed his mind.

It was true that no one had been having much fun around here. Not since Mom and Dad lost their jobs and couldn't find new ones.

If Arnie was a nice kid, he'd realize our parents had more on their minds than having fun.

But he's not nice.

The family meeting ended with Mom and Dad telling Arnie to work really hard at being good. But he already had the AirPods back in his ears. I don't think he heard a word.

Arnie disappeared to his room, and I helped clean up the dinner dishes. When we were finished, I followed Mom to the living room. "I need a baby picture," I told her. "Where are the baby pictures?"

"For Photo Day?" Mom asked.

I nodded. "Everyone has to bring in a baby photo. I need one that isn't too nerdy."

"Babies aren't nerdy," Mom said. "You were the cutest baby. Like a little princess."

"Gag me," I said, pushing my finger down my throat.

Mom laughed. "Don't start acting like your brother."

"I couldn't," I said. "I'm human."

"Follow me," Mom said. "To my laptop. I have all our family photos on flash drives. Go through them, and we'll print one out."

Dad was typing at the laptop on the table in their bedroom. "We need the laptop for a little while," Mom told him. "Amy has to do something for school."

Dad climbed to his feet. "Someday we'll all have our own laptops," he said. "Won't that be great?"

Mom pulled open the drawer under the table and lifted out a pile of flash drives. "I'm so organized. Are you impressed?" she said. "Each drive has a year written on the side."

"Very impressive," I said. I reached for the drive marked *2011*, the year I was born.

"No. Wait." Mom took it from my hand. "Even better. I made a separate flash drive for all the baby pictures." She handed me a drive with *Baby Pics* written in black marker on the side.

"Awesome," I said. I took the drive and slipped it into the side of the laptop. A few seconds later, I was gazing at all the old photos I had seen a million times.

Mom stood behind me with her hands on my shoulders, peering at the screen as I slid from photo to photo. "That's a cute one." She jabbed at the screen.

"With that jerky smile?" I said. "No way."

"Do you think you should look dignified in your baby pictures?" she asked.

I ignored the question. I knew what I was searching for. A photo the kids wouldn't make jokes about.

I scanned through the photos slowly. Here I was, starting to walk. Here I was, sitting in a little toy car.

There I was, in a high chair with chocolate ice cream smeared over my face.

Near the end of the file, I found a photo I liked. I was wearing bib overalls over a long-sleeved plaid shirt. I was sitting in a chair at a little table, holding a copy of *Pat the Bunny*, pretending to be reading.

"This one will work," I told my mom. "But wait. Let me finish the photo file. I'm almost at the end."

I leaned forward and scanned through more photos ... My first playdate with a girl I don't remember ... In a pointy party hat at someone's birthday party ... Naked in the bathtub. *Forget that one.*

I was nearly at the end when a thought flashed

into my mind. I scanned quickly, letting the photos slide by rapidly.

Then I stopped and turned to my mom. "Hey, weird," I said.

She squinted at me. "What's weird?"

"Well . . . did you say these were all the family baby pictures?"

"Yes. They are," she replied.

"Well, where are Arnie's baby photos?" I demanded. "Why aren't there any pics of Arnie in here?"

CHAPTER 10

SPLASH

"I put Arnie's baby photos on a separate flash drive," Mom said.

"You divided us up?" I said.

"You know how organized I am, Amy. I didn't have anything to do one day, and it seemed like a nice project."

I stared at her. "But what about all the photos where Arnie and I are together?" I asked.

"I put those on a third flash drive," she replied. "Want to see them?" She opened the drawer and began to sort through the dozens of flash drives.

"That's okay," I said. "Some other time. I found the photo I want to take to school. Let me just print it." I clicked *print*, and the printer hummed to life.

She closed the drawer.

"I still think separating the baby photos is weird," I said.

She frowned at me. "It isn't weird, Amy. Lots of people organize their photos. I'm just more organized than most."

I pulled the photo from the printer. Then I stood up and started to leave the room. But Mom followed me.

"Amy, can you do me a big favor?"

Uh-oh. Whenever she asks for a big favor, it always has to do with Arnie.

"Can you walk Arnie to school tomorrow morning? I have a job interview first thing, and I really want to prepare for it."

"Sure, Mom," I replied. Did I really have a choice? "But . . . remember last time?"

She sighed. "Yes, I remember. I'll make Arnie promise he won't do anything like that."

I rolled my eyes. "Like he ever keeps his promises," I murmured.

The last time I walked Arnie to school, he ran off and hid beneath someone's car that was parked on the street.

Big joke, right? I shouted for him till my voice was hoarse. And I searched everywhere. But he didn't come out.

I only found him when the car's owner decided to move it. And then I was half an hour late to my school.

"Maybe I could put him on a dog leash," I said.

Mom shook her head. "Enough, Amy. I know his behavior has been getting worse. But that kind of talk doesn't help matters."

She followed me into the hall. "One more thing."

I turned back to her.

"Are you and Lissa planning your weekly baking session for Saturday morning?"

Lissa and I love to bake. Mostly breads and little cakes and cookies. And we're pretty good at it.

"We're making banana bread on Saturday," I told Mom.

"That's perfect," Mom replied. "Can you bake an extra one I can take to Aunt Helen's? She loves banana bread."

"No problem," I said. "But Max can't have any." I was still angry with him for helping ruin my sleepover.

I walked into my room and closed the door. Arnie was in his room next door, screeching at the top of his lungs, singing along with blasting music. I could still hear him with my door closed. But I knew better than to ask him to make it quieter. He'd blast it even louder.

My phone buzzed with a text from Lissa. I picked it up and gazed at three baby pictures she had sent along with her message.

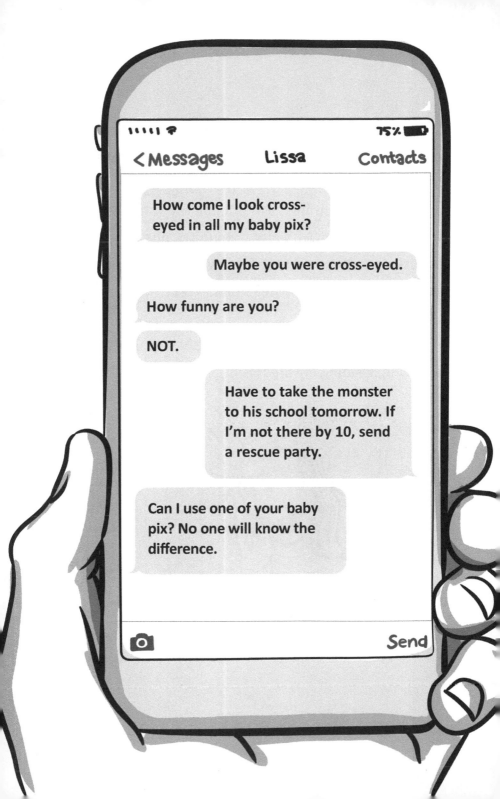

Funny idea.

I was still chuckling about it later as I lay in bed, covers pulled up to my chin. The afternoon storm had grown stronger. I listened to the pouring rain and watched lightning flash outside my window. It was a noisy storm, with lots of thunder, but I finally fell asleep. I dreamed that Arnie was crawling into my bedroom window instead of Max, singing at the top of his lungs.

My alarm went off, and I woke up shaking. The kid was even invading my dreams!

After breakfast, Arnie and I stepped out into a gray day. The rain had finally stopped, but dark clouds still hung low overhead. Cold raindrops fell from the trees as we walked under them.

A black SUV rumbled past, sending waves of water up over the curb on both sides. Arnie and I stepped in and out of the street to avoid the wide puddles on the sidewalk.

I shivered as a burst of wind sent raindrops into my face. I pulled my rain poncho tighter. It was the new poncho Aunt Helen had sent for my birthday.

This was the first time I'd worn it. It was light tan and very sophisticated. More like a trench coat, with a belt and everything.

We crossed Plum Street and made our way onto the school block. Arnie was being quiet. I decided to try to talk to him.

"What are you doing in school?" I asked.

"Minding my own business."

That was the end of *that* conversation.

We stopped at the edge of an enormous mud puddle that flooded the sidewalk. "Wow. It's like a lake," I said.

Arnie's eyes flashed. "Bet I can jump over it," he said.

I shook my head. "No way. Don't even try it."

"I can jump over it easy," he insisted. He backed up several steps. "Watch."

"No, Arnie—" I pleaded. "Don't try it. I mean it. Don't. I know what you're going to do."

"What am I going to do, Amy?"

"You're going to splash me," I said. "You're going to splash me and ruin my new poncho."

Arnie shook his head. "No way." He raised his right hand. "I swear. I can jump this puddle easily."

"No. Please—don't!" I cried.

He took a running start, bent his knees—and jumped.

SPLAAAAASH.

The little jerk jumped into the *middle* of the puddle. He didn't even try to jump the whole way over it.

I screamed and staggered back. But I wasn't fast enough. A high wave of mud splattered my new rain poncho. The wet mud oozed down the coat to my ankles and over my shoes.

"Arnie—you . . . you beast!" I wailed.

But he was laughing too hard to hear me.

CHAPTER 11

THE MONSTER ATTACKS!

By now, I guess you're getting a pretty good idea of my life with Arnie.

He ruined my sleepover with my friends and scared everyone to death. Now, Marta and Sophie won't come to my house.

He sent the script we needed to rehearse our musical flying out the window. And now he deliberately ruined my new rain poncho.

You probably think that's when I snapped. That's when I did the horrible thing to Arnie that changed our lives forever.

Well, you're wrong.

It gets much, much worse. Trust me.

After school, I found Mom in the kitchen. She was at the table with a dozen color-ful origami animals spread out in front of her.

Mom is very artistic. She's always painting and weaving things and making wall hangings. Before she lost the job, she had worked in a framing store because she liked to be close to art.

I stepped up to the table and examined an origami giraffe. "What are these for?"

"A charity thing," she said. Then her eyes went wide as she saw my rain poncho. "Oh, wow, Amy. What happened?"

I groaned. "Arnie happened," I said.

She grabbed the raincoat sleeve. "Did you fall?"

"No. I just told you. Arnie did it. He splashed me. Deliberately."

Her eyes moved down the wide, muddy stain. "Are you sure he did it on purpose?"

"Am I sure he's an animal?" I replied.

Mom frowned. "That's not helpful," she said softly. "Calling him names won't help."

"But what *will* help?" I cried. "Mom, Arnie is ruining my life!"

She picked up a square of blue construction

paper and began folding it. "And it doesn't help to exaggerate."

"How am I exaggerating?" I replied. "Look at this new poncho. Look at it."

She kept her eyes on the bird she was folding between her fingers. "I saw it. We know Arnie has problems—"

"Problems? I have the problems!" I shouted. I slammed the tabletop, and the paper animals all jumped. "Mom, you have to do something about him."

"Your brother is very difficult," she said. "We know that. Your dad and I are trying to do our best with him."

"Well, you're not doing *enough*!" I cried. "You heard him at our family meeting. He didn't take it

seriously for one minute. He thinks everything he says and does is a riot. And he doesn't care—"

Mom messed up the origami bird. She crumpled it into a ball and tossed it onto the table. "I know. I know, Amy. But give us a break. Your dad and I are under a lot of pressure. Our big worry is finding jobs." She sighed. "The money . . . it's running out."

I opened my mouth to reply but stopped myself. What could I say?

Mom tugged my sleeve again. "I have more bad news."

I rolled my eyes. "Now what?"

"I need you to babysit Arnie Saturday morning."

I started to take off my poncho but stopped. "But you know Lissa is coming over to bake our banana bread."

"Make the bread in the afternoon," she replied. "The two of you can take Arnie to the mall in the morning. Keep him busy. It's just a couple of hours. Then you can come back and make the bread."

Mom stared at me wide eyed with this pleading, pouty look on her face. *No way* I could say no to her.

"Where is Arnie anyway?" I asked. "Is he home?"

She shook her head. "Your dad had to go pick him up at soccer practice. The coach won't let him play anymore."

"Huh?" I cried. "Why not? What did he do?"

"He kept kicking the ball at the other kids' faces. On purpose. He gave two kids bloody noses."

"Mom, you have *got* to get him more help," I said.

She sighed. "I know. I know. But . . . we really can't afford another doctor now."

The front doorbell rang.

I hurried to answer it. "Sophie! Hi!"

She was dressed in a big maroon sweatshirt over black tights. Her hair was a frizz of curls from the wet, humid air.

She squinted at the stain on my poncho. "Amy, did you fall in the mud?"

"No," I said. "I got splashed."

"Why are you wearing it in the house? Does the ceiling leak?"

"I just got home," I said. "What's up, Sophie?"

"I thought maybe you could help me with my

science notebook. I got behind because I was sick last week, and I haven't been able to catch up."

I squinted at her. She wasn't carrying anything, and she wasn't wearing a backpack. "Well, where's your science notebook?"

"On the way here, I remembered I forgot it. I left it at home." She shrugged. "Can I take yours home with me?"

"Not a good idea," I said. "I need it tonight. I'll come over with it now and help you copy it."

"Thanks!" she said.

I grabbed my backpack and stepped outside, closing the front door behind me. "Sophie, can we just walk for a little while? I need some fresh air. Arnie has been a beast again and—"

"Sure." She moved aside so I could get down the front steps. We walked side by side down the driveway.

The lawns were still glistening wet from the rain. But the puddles were smaller, and we edged around them as we reached the sidewalk.

"Jared has been horrible, too," Sophie said.

I laughed. A bitter laugh. "Your little brother Jared

is an angel compared to mine. Does he spend his whole life trying to scare everyone and mess them up? No way."

"Jared chewed off all the tips on my colored pencils," Sophie said. "Does that count?"

"A minor crime," I said. "Not even worth mentioning it."

We turned onto Plum Street and passed the library and the elementary school playground. Some kids were still kicking a ball around on the soccer field. But, of course, Arnie was gone.

Sophie and I don't take walks very often, but I really enjoyed it. For one thing, Sophie knows all the gossip from school, and I knew her stories would take my mind off Arnie.

It was fun to stroll around the neighborhood and complain about our brothers and hear Sophie's gossip about the kids in our class.

Like Ricky Mendoza, who keeps a kitten in his dresser drawer that his parents don't know about. And Lacy Saltzman, who got caught at Target with two candy bars in her bag and told the manager they must have fallen off the shelf. And Adam Barker, who still eats his boogers even though he's twelve.

Lots to talk about. And it really did help take my mind off Arnie and how he was ruining every day of my life.

The afternoon sun was lowering behind the trees when I dropped Sophie off at her house. "It's kind of late. Can we go over the science notebooks tomorrow?" I asked.

She shrugged. "Maybe. Or maybe I'll just fake it." She laughed. "It might be easier." Then she disappeared into her house.

I cut through some backyards, then made my way onto my block. Some kids zoomed toward me on electric scooters. "Hey—!" I had to leap off the sidewalk to avoid getting run over. There was *no way* they were going to slow down.

I was halfway up my driveway when the thing came bursting out from the back of the house. A black blur, moving fast, low to the ground.

It took my eyes a few seconds to focus on it—and then I froze.

A big animal. An ugly creature. With a long purple beak like a bird and short antlers poking up from its head.

A different animal. Not the one I'd seen in my house.

Red eyes glowing. Snapping its beak. Galloping on all fours across the lawn. Coming straight for me.

CHAPTER 12

LICKING THE SQUIRREL

A wave of panic froze me on the spot.

I opened my mouth to scream, but no sound came out.

Did the ugly creature come out of the woods?

I'd never seen anything like it.

Its antlered head was lowered as it attacked. The long beak snapped loudly.

A monster. I was staring at another monster.

How could that be?

Was something strange going on in the woods?

No time to think about it. The creature snapped its beak again.

My house was so close. Just up the driveway. Could I somehow dodge around it and make it to the front door?

No. No way.

I had no choice. I spun away from it. Tried to run. My shoes slipped on the wet grass.

I stumbled to the sidewalk. Splashed through a puddle of leftover rainwater. Caught my balance. Burst into the street. Ducked alongside a parked car. And kept running.

My shoes slapped the pavement. My wheezing breaths nearly drowned out the creature's heavy footsteps.

I glanced back—just as it leaped into the air.

"Noooooo!" A scream of fear escaped my throat.

The creature bumped me hard from behind. Its purple beak clamped down on my leg. I heard my pants rip.

Struggling to catch my breath, I tried to wriggle free. But the monster didn't let go.

It held on tighter.

"Owwwww!" My leg. Pain shot up my side.

I stumbled forward. Tried to kick the big beast off me.

Then, to my surprise, it let go.

It dropped back to the street. And turned away from me.

My heart pounding, I backed up, watching it.

Something had caught the creature's attention.

It darted quickly to the grass. With a grunt, it stretched its front paws out—and grabbed a squirrel.

The squirrel kicked hard. But the monster held tight and raised it to its open beak.

Gripping its prey by the head and paws, the big creature stretched the small animal out.

The terrified squirrel uttered a shrill "*Eee-eee-eee.*"

The monster lifted the squirrel to its beak. A fat pink tongue shot out. And it *licked* the squirrel's belly from top to bottom.

"*Eee-eee-eee.*"

The squirrel continued its terrified cry.

Run! Now's your chance to escape! I thought. But I couldn't take my eyes off the creature.

As I gaped in horror and disbelief, the monster licked the squirrel again . . . licked its fur . . . licked it . . . licked it.

The monster stood upright on the grass and kept licking the squirrel with its long fat tongue. All the while, it kept its eyes on me.

Then, suddenly, it pulled the terrified little creature away from its beak—and flung it away. Heaved it across the grass.

Growling, the monster lowered its head—and began to scrabble over the grass. Coming for me. Coming for me again.

Run!

Run now!

I spun around and dove across the street without looking. A car horn blasted a long warning. Too late.

I heard the squeal of brakes. The loud skid of tires scraping the pavement.

I hit the street hard. And shut my eyes. I knew it was all over for me.

CHAPTER 13

ATTACK

I didn't move. I didn't breathe. After a long, dark moment, I opened my eyes. I glimpsed the front of a blue SUV inches from my body.

"Hey! Don't you watch where you're going?" An angry scream from the car.

A man burst out of the driver's side. "Are you okay? I didn't hit you. You fell in front of my car. Can you get up?"

With a groan, I pushed myself to my knees.

I wasn't hit. I wasn't hurt.

"Sorry," I called. I climbed to my feet. "I'm so sorry."

I turned to the curb. "Did you see the creature?" I cried. "It chased me into the street. Did you see it?"

"Huh? Creature? Are you messing with me?" He hurried back to his car. "You're okay, right? You're okay? Be careful," he called. "I'm sorry. I'm late. But you look okay." The car sped away with a roar.

I brushed off my jeans—and screamed as the monster rumbled out from behind a shrub. Breathing noisily, it lowered its head again and headed right for me, its heavy paws pounding the grass.

My legs suddenly felt as if they weighed two hundred pounds each.

But I forced myself to move.

I started to run and found myself back at Sophie's house. I raced up the lawn and leaped up the front steps two at a time. I raised both fists and pounded as hard as I could on the door.

"Sophie! Help me! Heeeeelp me!" My voice rang out high and shrill. "Help me! Hurry!"

The door swung open, and Sophie stood there, blinking at me in confusion. "Amy? What's wrong? What happened to your pants? The leg is torn!"

I was breathing too hard to answer. I lowered my shoulder and pushed into the hallway, sweeping her out of my way. "Help . . . I need help . . ."

"Are you okay? Are you sick? What's wrong?" she demanded.

I closed the front door behind me. "It . . . it was chasing me," I stammered.

Her eyes went wide. "Huh?"

"A monster . . ." I choked out. "It . . . it's still out there. I know it is!"

Sophie swept past me into the front room and hurried to the window. I followed, still trembling.

The drapes were pulled. I reached for the edge of the drapes with a trembling hand. I slid it open an inch and peered into the front yard with one eye.

I didn't see the monster. Was it hiding?

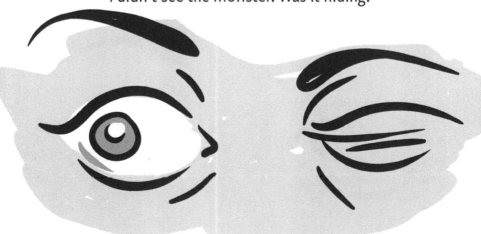

I pulled the drapes apart one more inch. I tried to keep myself hidden as I looked out.

Sophie leaned over me. "I don't see anything," she said.

I pulled the drapes open another inch. Then I cupped my hands around my eyes and squinted hard into the gray evening.

No sign of the creature.

I glanced up and down the block. Stared at the yards across the street. Moved my gaze to Sophie's front steps.

"Is it . . . really gone?" I gasped.

Sophie hugged herself. "Amy, you're scaring me," she said in a whisper. "Did you really see it? The animal from your house?"

My throat ached. I swallowed. "It—it wasn't the animal from my house. This was a different one," I replied. "This one had a long beak like a bird and antlers and . . . and . . . I fell and almost got killed running across the street."

"A different animal?" Sophie gasped and grabbed my arm.

We both stared into the gray late-afternoon light. We didn't speak for a long moment.

Sophie finally spoke in a whisper. "The animal at the sleepover last Friday . . ." she started. "We didn't see it. You're the only one who saw it."

"So?" I said.

"Well . . . I don't see anything out there now. You're the only one—"

"Are you saying that I'm making these up?" I cried. "Are you saying I'm imagining them?"

Sophie blinked. "No. But . . . you don't really believe there are two monsters on the loose in our neighborhood—do you?"

I felt a stab of anger. "I know what I saw," I said through clenched teeth. "I'm not making up a story just to scare you, if that's what you think."

"No, Amy. I—"

"What about the long black quills?" I demanded. "The quills on the pizza? You saw those, Sophie. They were real."

She thought about it for a moment. "That could have been one of Arnie's tricks," she said.

"Arnie was in his room, remember?" I tugged the drapes shut. "I saw this one clearly today. A totally different creature. It came from behind my house. Running on all fours, snapping its beak at me. It bit my leg . . . tore my pants." I showed her the hole in my jeans.

"Maybe they ripped when you fell?" Sophie's eyes were locked on mine. I could see she was studying me, trying to make up her mind about the strange animal.

I let out a long sigh and started to the front door. "I have to go home. I have to ask my parents if they saw anything."

"Are you sure you want to walk?" Sophie asked. "We could call your parents to come pick you up."

"That's okay," I said. "The creature is gone. My house is only two blocks away."

"Well . . ." Sophie hesitated.

"I'll text you when I get home," I said. "If you don't hear from me, you'll know I'm in trouble."

I pulled open the front door. A burst of cool evening air greeted me. I stepped onto the stoop. Sophie stood close behind me in the doorway.

I moved down the stairs and onto the front walk.

And let out a shuddering cry as the creature hit me from behind.

I felt its hard animal paws crash into my back. A powerful shove—and I went stumbling onto the grass.

CHAPTER 14

SHOULD WE BE SCARED?

"Skippy—get down! Skippy!" Sophie shouted.

I spun around to see a big yellow-and-white collie, its tail wagging furiously. It leaped on me again, stabbing me in the stomach with its big front paws.

"Skippy—stop!" Sophie cried. She jumped off the stoop and hurried over to pull the dog back.

"It's the neighbors' dog," she said, wrapping her arms around its neck. "He's way too friendly. He gets excited when he sees anyone, and he jumps on them."

"He—he surprised me," I stammered, tugging my jacket back into place. "I thought—"

She hugged the dog for a while longer, then let him go. His tail wagged back and forth like a windshield wiper, and he gazed up at me with his mouth open. But he had finished his jumping.

"Good boy, Skippy," Sophie said. "He still thinks he's a puppy. He doesn't know how big and strong he is."

I realized I was still breathing hard. I took a long, deep breath and held it. Then I let it out.

"Thanks for the greeting, Skippy," I said. "Sophie, I've got to get home."

I gave her a quick wave, then started walking down the front lawn on shaky legs.

I was a block from my house when I saw the kids on electric scooters again. I waved them to a stop. Two boys and a girl, about Arnie's age.

"I saw you guys before," I said. "I live in that house up there." I pointed.

"I know your brother," the girl said. "He's in my class."

"He's weird," one of the boys said.

All three kids laughed.

"Were you on this block earlier?" I asked. "Did you see me running across the street? Did you see some kind of creature chasing after me?"

"Creature?" one of the boys said. "You mean like an animal?"

"Kind of," I replied. "Did you see it?"

They shook their heads. "We didn't see an animal," the girl said.

"Was it a coyote?" one of the boys asked. "My dad said we have to watch out for coyotes. They come out of the woods and—"

"No. Not a coyote," I told him. I gazed at my house. "Okay," I said. "I've got to get home." I walked past them. "Take care, guys."

My eyes darted left and right. I was on high alert as I made my way up the driveway toward the door. But I saw Arnie and Dad in the yard.

They were kicking a soccer ball back and forth. "Hey—!" I called out and hurried over to them.

"Where've you been?" Dad asked. "I'm trying to teach your brother how to kick a soccer ball without smashing it into someone's face."

"I didn't do it on purpose!" Arnie cried. He kicked the ball against the wooden fence at the side of the yard. "It was an accident!"

"An accident *five times*?" Dad cried. "That was a lot of accidents." He turned to me. "Coach Garcia said he doesn't want Arnie on the team."

"Maybe Arnie thought he was playing dodgeball," I said. It was a joke, but they didn't laugh.

"Everyone has accidents," Arnie said, kicking the ball against the fence again. "Why does everyone pick on me?"

I grabbed Dad's arm. "I have to talk to you. Did you see anything back here? A weird creature came running from here and—"

He frowned at me. "A weird creature?" he said. "What kind of weird creature? Another monster?"

"Dad, let me finish," I pleaded. "Yes. Another monster. You have to believe me. It chased after me. Chased me down the street and—"

Dad moved his hands to my shoulders. "Amy, please. Stop with the monster talk."

"It's real, Dad. I—I was so scared—"

He locked his eyes on mine. "Did anyone else see it?"

"No, but—"

"Amy, you're the only one seeing these animals." He shook his head. "I'm really getting worried about you. I know it's my fault, but . . ."

"Your fault?" I said. "Why?"

"For showing you that scary movie when you were too little," he answered. "It scared you to death, and now you're suddenly seeing monsters everywhere."

"Dad, I really *like* scary movies!" I exclaimed. "I'm not scared because of a movie. I'm scared because I saw *real monsters*!"

Arnie stepped between Dad and me. He tossed the ball across the grass. "Amy, can I tell you the truth?" he said. A grin spread over his face. "The monster that chased you? It was me. I was the monster."

Dad laughed.

"Nice try," I said. "But the monster wasn't that ugly."

Arnie shrugged. Then he curled his hands up like claws in front of his face and did a fierce lion growl at me. "Did I scare you?"

"I'm shaking all over." I turned to Dad. "I'm not imagining things," I said. "I know what I saw. I—"

The kitchen door opened and Mom poked her head out. "Dinnertime," she shouted. "I made your favorites. Fish eyes and chicken thumbs."

She likes to make up funny foods. She's actually pretty good at it.

Arnie tried to trip me as I began trotting to the house. I shoved him away with one shoulder bump.

"Mom says you and Lissa are taking me to the mall tomorrow," he said.

"Yeah. If you promise to behave," I said.

"Behave? Is that a word?" He laughed.

"Promise," I said.

"Can we go to Game Haven? You don't have to buy me anything. They let you play the games there for free."

"Maybe," I said.

I shivered thinking about having to spend time with Arnie at the mall. I didn't realize that Lissa and I were about to learn something very surprising about him.

CHAPTER 15

CALL FOR THE MALL POLICE

"Arnie—get out of the fountain! What are you *doing*?"

Lissa and I dove forward. We grabbed him by the arms and lifted him out of the water fountain, kicking and giggling.

It was early Saturday morning. The mall was nearly empty. But a few people, staring in surprise, turned and watched us struggle with him.

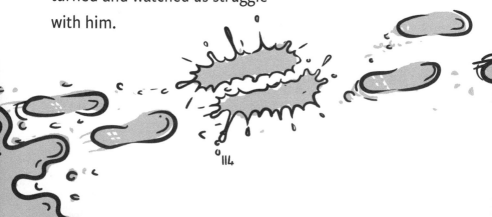

"Stop kicking!" Lissa cried. "You're getting us totally wet!"

We set him down but held on to him. "Why did you walk into the fountain?" I demanded. "Did you think that was funny?"

"Pretty funny," he said.

I shook him by the shoulders. "But you promised—"

"You mean it isn't for swimming?" He laughed.

The cuffs of his jeans were soaked, as well as his shoes and socks.

"Look at you," I said. "You're going to have to walk around the mall completely wet."

Lissa pointed. "See those people staring at you?" she asked. "They can't believe you walked into the fountain."

"I don't care," he said. "I wanted to make a wish."

"Give us a break," I said. "You know that isn't how you make a wish. You throw a penny in to make a wish."

"Well, I didn't have a penny," Arnie replied. "So I threw myself in."

His shoes squished on the tile floor as he began to walk away from us.

"Where are you going?" I demanded. Lissa and I hurried to catch up to him.

A white-haired woman leaned over a perfume cart in the middle of the aisle. She turned to us as we chased after Arnie. "Problem child?" she said.

"You can say *that* again," I replied.

"I'll pray for you," she said.

I could see where my brother was headed. The Game Haven store stood across from the Cinnabon counter and a pharmacy.

I ran in front of Arnie and stuck my arms out to block his path. "You can go in there," I said. "But you have to promise to be good. Otherwise—"

He gave me a thumbs-up.

"Do you promise? Say it out loud," I demanded.

"I promise I'll be as good as I can be," he said with that typical grin. He raised his right hand. "I swear."

Lissa sighed. "He's lying."

I knew she was right, but what choice did we have? At least Game Haven would keep him busy for a while.

On the way to the mall, I had told Lissa about the second monster. Of course, I couldn't stop thinking about it.

"It chased me into the street. I was almost killed," I said.

Lissa stared at me. Her face was blank.

"You don't believe me?" I demanded.

"I don't believe in monsters," she replied. "You're stressed, Amy. You're imagining—"

"Stop!" I covered her mouth with my hand. "Just stop. I won't talk about monsters anymore."

I decided not to mention monsters again. At least not today.

It was still early when we stepped into Game Haven. I saw two store clerks, a young man and a woman in matching red-and-white Hawaiian shirts.

They were still setting up the counter displays. Screens around the store silently showed previews of different video games.

The two clerks turned when we came in. "Can we help you find anything?" the woman asked.

Arnie pointed to a screen across the store. "I want to try that game, *Alien Battle Heroes*."

"Have you played it before?" she asked.

"Maybe," he answered.

She raised her eyes to us. "Is it okay if he plays it for a while?"

"Please," I said. "If it isn't too much trouble."

She walked over to the monitor and picked up a controller from the counter beside it. She pressed several buttons, and the game rebooted on the screen.

Arnie walked over, and she handed him the game controller. He squinted at the screen. "I don't want to play level one," he told her. "I'm on level six."

"Arnie, be polite," I said.

"I *am* being polite," he answered. "Why do I have to play level one?"

The store clerk's name tag read FRANNY. Franny pushed more buttons on the controller. Then she handed it back to him. "There you go. Level six."

Arnie didn't say thank you or anything. He turned to the screen and began to destroy alien warriors.

After a few minutes and several noisy, screaming attacks, he paused the game. "You two can leave," he said to Lissa and me. "I'll be playing for a while."

"I don't think so," I said. "Lissa and I are going to keep an eye on you."

He grinned. "You don't trust me?"

"Of course not," Lissa answered.

He went back to the game and began blasting away.

Franny turned to me. "He looks like trouble," she said.

"He *is* trouble," I replied.

She held up a box. "The new *Sonic the Hedgehog* just came in. He might like to try it."

"I don't think so," I said. "He only likes games where he can destroy things."

She nodded and returned to the other store clerk. He was struggling to hang a *World of Pain* poster on the wall.

Lissa and I wandered around the store for a while. We're not into video games, so the place wasn't very interesting to us.

While Arnie crushed aliens, we stopped near the door and talked about the banana bread recipe. "I have three very ripe bananas," I said. "I think that should be enough."

"If we make two breads, we can keep one for us," Lissa said.

"I don't think my parents have two loaf pans," I said. "I could only find one, and—"

I stopped when Arnie let out a cry. "I'm up to level eight," he said. "This game is so awesome!"

"Glad you're enjoying it," I said. "Wrap it up. We have to go soon."

"Hey—buy this game for me," he shouted across the store.

Lissa and I moved closer. "Buy it?" I said. "No way."

"Buy it for me! You have Mom's card."

I frowned at him. "You know we didn't come here to buy anything, Arnie. We came here so you could play for a while. Anyway, be patient. Your birthday is in a couple of weeks."

His eyes lit up. "You'll buy it for my birthday?"

"Maybe," I said. "We'll see."

Lissa glanced at her phone. "We should get going."

"No way!" Arnie cried. "One more level. One more." He grabbed the controller and turned back to battle more space warriors.

Lissa and I moved behind him and watched. When he finished the level with a loud burst of his laser blaster, I grabbed him by the shoulders. "Let's go. Don't start another level."

He dragged his feet behind us as we headed to the front of the store.

Franny greeted us at the door. She smiled at Arnie. "You're very good at that game," she said. "Hope they buy it for you."

"Yeah. Hope so," he muttered.

"Just one more thing," she said. She reached a hand toward my bag. "I'm sorry. Can I see what's in there?"

"Huh?" I stared at her. "My bag? Why?"

"Your bag," she repeated. "Please open it for me."

I stood there with my mouth hanging open.

Franny quickly slid her hand into my bag and pulled out a game box.

"Oh nooooo," Lissa and I both moaned together.

"Whoa!" Arnie cried. "How did *that* get in there?"

"Arnie—what did you *do*?" I cried.

My heart jumped up to my throat. I grabbed Franny's arm. "I'm not a thief!" I cried. "I swear. I didn't do it!"

Franny moved to block the front door. She pulled out a phone. "I'm really sorry," she said. "We have a very strict shoplifting policy. I have to call the mall police."

CHAPTER 16

THE ORANGE SMOOTHIE

"Did you take it for *me*?" Arnie asked.

"Are you kidding me?" I cried. "No way."

I turned back to Franny. "You believe me—don't you? You know I wasn't the one who put it in my bag?"

She stared hard at me and didn't answer.

Am I really going to be arrested? I thought.

Is Arnie really going to get me arrested for shoplifting?

"Tell you what," Franny said, turning to me. "I believe you. I have a little brother at home. He's a total jerk, too."

She pushed open the door. "Go ahead. You can go. But you can't come back here," she told Arnie.

"Hey, thanks," I said.

Arnie marched out the door without saying a word to her.

I thanked her again, and we started to walk. "Why didn't you thank Franny for letting you go?" I asked.

"Because she called me a jerk," Arnie said.

"You *are* a jerk," Lissa said.

"You're more than a jerk," I said. "You could have gotten me arrested. I could be sent to prison! I—I—I—"

He laughed. "Lighten up. I almost got away with it."

You probably think this is where I totally lost it.

I mean, Arnie the thief tried to make it look like I was shoplifting a game. Franny almost called the mall police. I almost went to jail.

You probably think that was the last straw. That this was when I cracked.

But hang on. That's nothing. There's more.

And believe me, the things Arnie did to me after this were so bad, I had no choice.

I had to get revenge. I just didn't know how frightening my revenge would be.

But trust me. We're not there yet.

I checked my phone as we walked through the mall. It was still too early to take Arnie home. I promised Mom we'd keep him here till at least noon.

Someone had left an empty soda can on the floor. He ran up to it and kicked it as hard as he could. It bounced off a shop window and startled two little girls who were sitting on a bench. They both screamed.

That made Arnie laugh.

I grabbed his shoulder. "Are you going to do anything *good* today?" I asked.

"I don't understand the question," he said.

"I *bet* you don't," I replied. "You don't know the word *good*—do you?"

He didn't answer. He ran up to the soda can and pulled his foot back to kick it again. But I grabbed him around the waist and tugged him back.

Lissa and I exchanged glances. I could read her face. She was saying, *What are we going to do with him? He's impossible.*

"Arnie, do you like smoothies?" Lissa asked. She pointed. "The Smoothie Shack is over there."

Arnie shrugged. "I guess. What flavors do they have?"

"Let's find out," Lissa replied.

"Can I have two?" he said.

"How about one?" I answered. "After what you just did . . ."

We stepped inside. The place was small and bright and smelled

like bananas. It had a long counter and red stools. Two teenage girls with white AirPods in their ears sat at the far end, the only other customers.

We dropped onto stools. The smoothie flavors were written on the mirrored wall behind the counter.

"They have piña colada," Lissa said. "I love piña colada."

"Me too," I said. "Arnie, do you want a piña colada, too?"

"Gag me," he said. He stuck a finger down his throat.

"Is that a no?" I said.

"I'll try orange," he said. "Supersize it."

A young man with curly red hair and freckles on his face stepped up on the other side of the counter. The badge on his white apron read *Keep It Smooth*.

"Good morning, guys," he said. He set down three paper cups of water. "What can I get you?"

"Two piña coladas and an orange," I said.

"Supersize it," Arnie said.

"Sorry. We only have one size." He held up a plastic cup to demonstrate.

"Why?" Arnie said.

The young guy made a face at Arnie and turned away. "I'll get your smoothies."

Arnie reached for his water cup, but I pulled his hand away. I knew what he was going to do. Spill it all over and pretend it was an accident. He does this in every restaurant we go to. And he thinks it's a riot every time.

"Hey—" he protested. "Give me the water. I'm thirsty."

"No, you're not," I said. "You just want to spill it on Lissa and me." I shoved the water cups out of his reach. "You've done enough this morning. Wait for your smoothie."

He drummed his fingers on the counter. Hard and loud.

"Do you have to do that?" I asked.

He nodded and kept drumming.

Luckily, the smoothies came before I strangled him.

He raised his cup, tilted it to his mouth, and poured half the smoothie down his throat, swallowing big gulps.

"Hey, what's your rush?" Lissa demanded.

He had an orange mustache above his lips. "I just decided I like orange smoothies," he answered. He took another long drink.

I took a sip of mine. It was thick and sweet and tasted like pineapple.

"What are we going to do next?" Arnie asked.

"We have to go home," I said. "Lissa and I have to bake banana bread."

I expected him to protest and argue. I expected

him to demand to go to the toy store and the cell phone store.

But he nodded and quietly murmured, "Okay."

He gulped down the rest of his orange smoothie. To my shock, he actually wiped his mouth with a napkin. He raised his blue eyes to me. "I want to say something," he said.

"Is it something rude?" I replied.

He shook his head. "I want to apologize to you both."

Lissa and I both gasped. "Huh? Apologize?"

"I'm really sorry about the game store," he said. "I never should have put that game in your bag. What was I *thinking*?"

I stared hard at him. Was he really *apologizing*?

It would be a first. I'd never heard Arnie apologize for anything in his entire life.

Lissa put her hand over his forehead. "Are you running a fever?"

"I'm serious," he said. "I'm really sorry. Can we go back and apologize to Franny?"

"Sure," I said. Lissa and I gazed at each other

above his head. *Is he sick? Is this some new kind of Arnie joke?*

"I don't want to be a jerk," he said, staring into the mirror. "I guess I have to try harder."

"We should get him to a hospital," Lissa said. "This is impossible."

The two teenage girls stood up at the other end of the counter. They walked behind us as they left the restaurant.

"Hey—" Arnie cried out and started to run to where they'd been sitting.

I saw what he was looking at. One of the girls had left her cell phone on the counter.

"No—!" I screamed. "Don't take that, Arnie. You can't have it!"

He grabbed the phone. I knew what he was going to say. *Finders keepers.*

I tried to grab it from him. But he dodged away from me and ran to the restaurant door. "Hey—you left your phone!" he shouted to the girls.

I stood in the doorway and watched him run after them. "You left your phone!" he cried.

The girl was so happy as he handed it to her. They both thanked him and patted him on the head and thanked him some more. Arnie had a big grin on his face as he came back into the restaurant.

Lissa paid for the smoothies. The three of us walked back out into the mall. It was nearly lunchtime and starting to get more crowded.

Suddenly, Arnie took off running. I saw where he was going. He had spotted the soda can still on the floor.

I waited for him to kick it again. But he picked up the can, carried it to a trash basket, and tossed it in.

Lissa poked me in the ribs. "Did you see that?"

"I saw it," I replied. "But I don't believe it."

She watched Arnie come running back to us. "We learned something interesting about your brother today."

I squinted at her. "What do you mean?"

"Orange smoothies change his whole personality."

"Do you think?"

She nodded. "Yes. Definitely. You should order a dozen of them to go."

Was Lissa right? It was hard to believe.

But Arnie was an angel all the way home. Of course, it didn't last.

That afternoon, he was a nightmare again.

CHAPTER 17

FROM UNDER A ROCK

"I found two loaf cake pans," I said. "So should we just double the recipe?"

Dad took the page I had printed out from the online recipe app. "Sure. Just double it." He glanced down at the ingredients Lissa and I had spread out on the kitchen counter. "Do you have everything?"

"I think so," Lissa said. "Let's go over it." She took the page from my dad and read the list, one by one. "Flour, baking soda . . ."

I shook the box. "Not much left."

"You don't need much," Dad said.

"Salt . . . butter . . . brown sugar . . ." Lissa continued.

I picked up the brown sugar box and studied it. "It says it expired two years ago."

"That's okay," Dad said. "Brown sugar doesn't go bad."

"Eggs," Lissa read. "That's it. We've got it all."

Dad chuckled. "What about bananas?"

"Oh! Yes. Bananas!" I cried. "We bought ripe bananas." I began to search. "Where did we put them?"

"I ate them," Arnie said, stepping into the kitchen.

"You *what*?" I cried.

"I ate them," he said. "Can I help it if I get hungry?"

Lissa gasped.

"You did not!" I said. I pulled the ripe bananas from the bread drawer at the bottom of the cabinet where I had stored them.

He made a disgusted face. "Yuck. Those are sick. I hate bananas."

"You just like lying," I said.

"Give your brother a break," Dad said.

"Why?" I replied.

Lissa squinted at the tall paper cup in Arnie's hand. One of the cups we use for popcorn on Family Movie Night. "What are you going to do with that, Arnie?"

"Wear it," he said.

"Can't you ever answer a question?" I asked.

"No," he said.

"Come on. What are you doing with the cup?" Dad asked.

"I'm going to barf into it. After I taste their banana bread."

"Stop it, Arnie!" Dad shouted. "What is the cup for?"

"Collecting things," Arnie answered. "Kwame and I are going to collect things from under rocks."

Kwame lives down the street. He is one of Arnie's few friends. They're in the same third-grade class. I don't know why he gets along so well with Arnie. Because no one else does.

"It's for school," Arnie said, heading to the kitchen door. "You know. For science. Discovering things under rocks."

"You came from under a rock," I told him.

That made Lissa laugh. Dad just shook his head.

The door slammed behind Arnie.

"You girls have fun," Dad said. He started to leave the kitchen. "Can't wait to taste it."

I know he doesn't like banana bread. He was just being nice. Dad always tries to be nice. Arnie definitely doesn't get his personality from Dad or Mom.

"How did Mom's job interview go?" I called after him.

"I haven't heard from her," he answered. He sighed. "That's not a good sign."

Lissa and I turned to the banana bread recipe. "What do we do first?" I asked.

"It says to combine the dry ingredients in one bowl."

I pulled a large mixing bowl from the shelf. "Dry ingredients," I said. "Is butter a dry ingredient?"

"I don't think so." Lissa studied the recipe sheet. "It says to beat the butter and sugar in another bowl. And then put in the eggs and the mashed-up bananas."

"Okay. I'll do that," I said. "You do the dry stuff." I pulled out the electric mixer for the wet ingredients. "Then what?"

"Then we add the dry mixture to the wet mixture, and we have the batter."

"Easy," I said.

"Piece of cake," Lissa murmured. I think it was a joke.

We started mixing ingredients. It didn't take long. When the dry stuff was all together, we added it to the wet stuff in the electric mixer and stirred every-thing together.

We were still stirring when Arnie burst through

the kitchen door. He raised the big paper cup in front of him. "Look what Kwame and I found."

"Not now," I said. "We're finishing up—"

"Hundreds of bugs crawling around under the rocks," he said. "Hundreds. Big ones. Look!"

"Not now—" I repeated.

He raised the cup in front of him.

"WHOOPS!"

He pretended to trip on a chair leg.

And dumped the entire cup of insects into our cake batter.

CHAPTER 18

MONDAY-MORNING SHOCK

"You can't punish him? What do you *mean*?" I cried.

"Please don't shout in the car," Dad said. "You know I have sensitive ears."

He and I were driving to the bakery in town to see if they had any banana bread. I'd never been so angry. My heart was beating hard, and my hands were clenched into tight fists in my lap. I couldn't calm down.

"Arnie has to be punished, Dad," I said through gritted teeth.

"He says it was an accident," Dad replied.

"Oh, give me a break!" I shouted. "Like stealing a video game and putting it in my bag was an accident! You and I both know he's lying." I let out an angry growl. "You can't let him get away with *everything*."

Dad spun the car into the bakery parking lot. "Your mom and I had a very honest talk with him."

"An honest talk? Big whoop," I muttered.

"We don't know what else to do," Dad said. He parked right in front of the shop. It was late afternoon, near closing time, and the bakery lot was empty.

"You could chain him to the wall in the basement and feed him nothing but bread and water for a week," I said.

Dad frowned at me. "We don't have a basement. Remember?"

"You could ground him for a year," I said.

"But then we'd be stuck with him in the house twenty-four hours a day, Amy. Total nightmare."

We climbed out of the car and walked to the bakery entrance. Dad stopped and turned to me at the door. "Believe me, I'm worried about Arnie," he said. "But I'm more worried that your mom and I don't have jobs. We'll deal with your brother. I promise. But we're mostly thinking about our money problem."

I squeezed his hand. "I get it, Dad. I'll just try to ignore Arnie this weekend. I'll try not to pay any attention to the little jerk."

He held the door open, and I led the way into the store. They didn't have any banana bread left. We had to settle for a walnut-raisin cake.

I kept my word. I ignored Arnie the rest of the weekend.

He came into my room a couple of times late on Saturday and tried to start a fight. But I pretended he wasn't there. "You're invisible," I told him. "So just go away."

"If I'm invisible, why are you talking to me?" he demanded.

I didn't answer.

On Sunday, he got the idea and stayed away from me. I think he was outside most of the day, turning rocks over with Kwame.

It was a peaceful day. Sophie, Lissa, and I hung out

for a while and talked about Photo Day on Monday and a bunch of other things.

I wanted to talk about the monsters with them. I kept picturing the creatures in my mind.

But when I started to talk about how I'm always looking over my shoulder now, I saw those blank looks on their faces again. I knew they didn't want to talk about the monsters.

I knew they wouldn't believe me.

We messed around with one another's hair. And Lissa dabbed on a bright-red lipstick that made her look like she was eating a tomato. A fun time.

Sunday night, I pulled the tunic dress from my closet. I held it up to me and studied it in the mirror on my closet door.

"What was I thinking?" I muttered to myself. "No way. Especially since it was Marta's old dress."

I jammed the dress back into the closet. I pulled out straight-legged black jeans and a creamy-white pullover top. Simple and perfect.

I thought I might have trouble falling asleep. I admit it, I was a little psyched for Photo Day.

But I drifted off a few minutes after my head hit the pillow, and I don't think I had any dreams.

I awoke the next morning to voices in the kitchen. Mom and Dad were having some kind of discussion.

The red morning sun poured through my bedroom window. I sat up and stretched. Were they arguing or just talking? They usually didn't say a word to one another until they'd had their coffee.

I stretched my arms above my head again. Then I climbed out of bed, pulled down my nightshirt, and walked barefoot down the hall to the kitchen.

They were both standing at the sink with white coffee mugs in their hands. "Morning," I muttered.

They turned. Both of them gasped. Their eyes went wide.

"OH NO!" Mom cried. "I don't believe it! OH NO!"

CHAPTER 19

THE LAST STRAW

"Wh-what's wrong?" I stammered.

They both gaped at me, their mouths hanging open.

"What's wrong?" I cried. "Why won't you speak?"

Mom shuddered. Dad shook his head. "Amy," he said, "did you look in the mirror before you came to the kitchen?"

"No," I said. "I heard you two talking and—"

Mom rushed forward and grabbed me by the shoulder. "I don't believe this," she said again. "I just don't." She took my hand. "Come with me."

"What's going on?" I cried.

"Just come with me." She pulled me into the bathroom and pushed me up to the mirror.

"Oh nooooo." A horrified moan escaped my lips. "How—? How—"

I stared at the thick black letters painted on my forehead. Black letters—two inches tall—spelling out a very rude word.

"Arnie!" I screamed. "Arnie! He . . . he did this to me!"

"I didn't even know Arnie *knew* this word," Mom said, biting her bottom lip.

I stared into the mirror, trying to fight back tears. "I'll kill him!" I cried. "Where is he? He knew it was Photo Day! I'll kill him!"

"He went to school early with Kwame," Mom said. "You and I can both kill him later. Let's wash that word off you."

She soaped a washcloth and waited for the water in the sink to get warm. I leaned over the sink, and she began to rub the black letters. After a while, she soaped the cloth again and began to rub harder.

"Ouch. Mom—leave some skin!" I cried.

"It's . . . not coming off," she said. She tossed down the washcloth. "We can try my makeup remover."

She turned to the door as Dad appeared. He raised his hand. It was wrapped around a fat black marker. "You won't believe this," he said. "Arnie used a permanent marker."

Mom and I both uttered cries.

Dad shook his head. "That's going to take a long time to come off," he said.

"But it's Photo Day—" I started.

"I'm so sorry, Amy," he said. "But you can't go to school with that word on your face."

I raised both fists above my head and screamed. "Why? Why did he do this?"

Dad thought for a long moment. "I think he was upset that you acted like he was invisible this weekend."

"You definitely can't go to school," Mom said. "Maybe they'll let you make up what you miss."

"Make up what I miss?" I cried. "Make up Photo Day? Are you out of your mind?"

"Okay, okay," Mom said, raising both hands. "Stop screaming. We have to find a way to be calm."

"I'm never going to be calm again!" I cried. I grabbed the washcloth and began scrubbing my forehead as hard as I could. "Never!"

"I know," Mom said. "We could wrap a bandanna around your forehead. Cover up the word, and you can go to school."

I rolled my eyes. "No way. I'm not going to have my photo taken in a stupid bandanna like I'm playing pirate or something. Should I get an eye patch, too? And put a parrot on my shoulder?"

"A bandanna could look cool," Dad said.

"No, it couldn't!" I shouted. "Only dogs wear bandannas!"

They both stared at me. I could see they were thinking hard. But they didn't have any answers.

"So sorry, Amy," Mom said finally. "You can't go anywhere with that word on your forehead. You'll have to stay home."

"We can call Dr. Krupp, the dermatologist," Dad said. "She knows everything about skin. I'm sure she'll know how to get the black ink off."

"Maybe I'll just leave it on FOREVER!" I cried. I shoved Dad out of the doorway and ran down the hall to my room.

I slammed the door behind me and ran to my bed. My cell phone was on the bed table. I grabbed it and took a selfie. My hand was shaking so hard I had to take it three times.

Then I texted it to Lissa.

Look at me. Arnie did this.

A few seconds later, I received her reply.

OMG OMG OMG.

My hands wouldn't stop shaking, but I managed to text her back.

> Can't come to school.
> I'm too obscene.

> We need to meet later.
> Maybe Sophie and Marta,
> too.

> This is the last straw. The
> END for Arnie. Seriously.
> The END.

> It's payback time.
> Time to plan a
> BIG-TIME REVENGE!

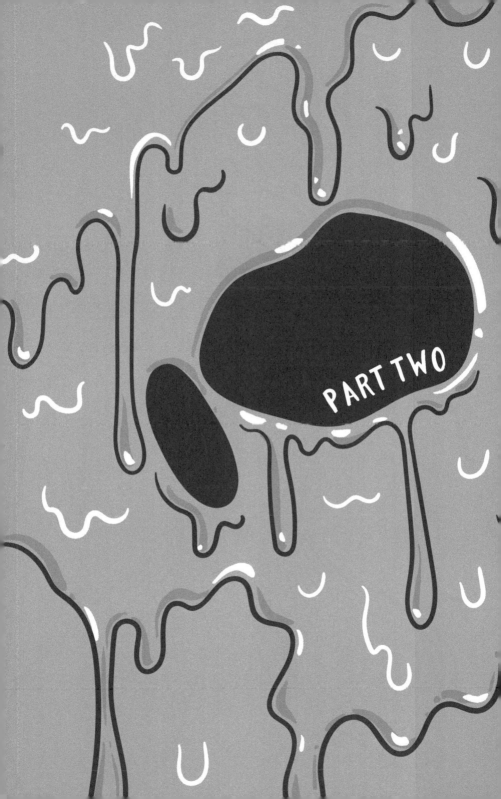

PART TWO

CHAPTER 20

A GOOD REVENGE?

Okay. Now you know.

Now you know what drove me over the edge. What made me finally decide to take matters into my own hands. To punish my awful brother. To take my REVENGE!

Every time I looked in the mirror, there was that word on my forehead.

Every time I looked in the mirror, my face would go red. I'd grit my teeth and clench my fists, and the anger would boil up from me like steam.

I knew it was time for REVENGE.

But here's what I didn't know—I didn't know that sometimes revenge can backfire . . .

"Why can't your parents just send Arnie to boarding school?" Marta said. "That's where my parents always threaten to send me whenever I do something they don't like." She rolled her eyes. "Like every day."

I laughed. "You're making that up."

"No. For real," Marta said. "But they'd never do it. Because then who would walk the dog in the afternoon? And who would empty the dishwasher? And who would fold the wash? And—"

"We can't afford to send Arnie to boarding school," I said. "It's expensive, isn't it?"

"I don't know anyone who went to boarding school," Sophie said. "Where is one anyway? Do we have any in Mayfair Falls?"

Lissa shrugged. "Beats me. Boarding school makes me think of Hogwarts."

"Well, we can't send Arnie to Hogwarts, even if it

was real," I said. "He'd like it too much. We have to think of something Arnie will hate."

Lissa frowned. "He'd probably cast spells on the other kids and ruin their faces, too."

"Hey! My face isn't ruined," I said.

"Then why do you have an inch of face makeup on your forehead?" Marta asked. "And why did you change your hair so you suddenly have those long bangs?"

I sighed. "The ink is fading. The word is coming off. You can hardly see it. It just looks like a smudge."

"Maybe we should draw really bad words all over Arnie's face," Sophie said. "You know. Get even."

I chuckled. "My parents would kill me."

"Anyway, that's not bad enough," Lissa said. "We need to do something to that little monster that will ruin his life forever."

That wasn't funny, but it made us all laugh.

"We could get his face tattooed red and blue," Lissa said. "My cousin Frankie works part-time at the tattoo place on Sandusky Street."

"Arnie would probably think that's cool," Marta said. "We need to think of a way to *terrify* him. Something he'll never forget."

We were all quiet for a while, thinking. Dreaming up the perfect revenge.

The four of us were sprawled on the thick navy-blue shag rug in Marta's den. It's an awesome room, nearly as big as my whole house. An enormous flat-screen TV hung on one wall. A marble fireplace wider than a garage door stood on the wall across from it. The couch and three big armchairs formed a semicircle in front of the TV. It was all heavy and dark, smooth blue leather, very old-fashioned looking.

I gazed at our shoes, lined up in the den doorway. We would never think of wearing shoes on the rug. Marta's parents were both clean freaks. They always seemed to be squinting around, searching for spots and stains.

Gilbert, their little white terrier, wasn't even allowed in most of the rooms.

Marta took a long sip from the water bottle she'd been cradling in her hands. "Would anyone mind if we just drowned Arnie?" she asked.

More laughter.

"My parents *might* mind," I said. "I'm not sure."

Sophie's eyes went wide. "We don't really want to *kill* him, do we?"

"No," Lissa told her. "That was a joke. We'd probably get in trouble if we killed him."

Everyone started talking at once. But I suddenly had an idea. I climbed onto my knees to get their attention.

"Listen. What do you think of this?" I said. "Arnie is a little monster, right? What if we somehow find one of the vicious creatures I saw last week and make it go after him? It could be awesome."

Lissa put a hand on my forehead. "Are you sick? I think you have a fever, Amy. Those creatures ... Those monsters are in your head. There *are* no monsters."

I tugged her hand away. "You're wrong, Lissa. Stop looking at me like that, Marta. You too, Sophie. The monsters are real. You all saw the quills in the oven. You saw—"

"We never saw any monster," Marta said. "Or any kind of animal."

"We searched everywhere for it," Sophie said. "It wasn't in your house. And I didn't see the second one either."

"You're the only one who has ever seen these monsters," Lissa said. "If they are real, why hasn't anyone in the neighborhood seen them?"

"I'm not making it up!" I screamed. I didn't mean to shout, but they were starting to totally annoy me. "Do you really not believe me?"

"You probably saw a couple of animals from the woods." Lissa tried to calm things down. "Sometimes animals come out when they're hungry. You know, looking for food," she said.

"But—but—" I sputtered.

"Even if the creatures you *think* are monsters are real," Marta said, "how do you plan to make one of them chase after your brother?"

"Okay, okay." I sank back to the rug. "Bad idea. I admit it. Bad idea. Can we just forget it?"

Sophie shivered. "I wish I could forget it. All that monster talk gave me nightmares last week."

"Stop being such a wimp!" I snapped.

Lissa punched my shoulder. "Don't start taking it out on Sophie. We're here to help you get even, re-member? We're not here to fight about it."

I turned to Sophie. "Sorry."

The four of us stared at one another for a while.

Then I remembered something. Something that could be the perfect revenge.

CHAPTER 21

SLIME TIME?

"I've got it," I said. "I think I have it. The perfect revenge."

They all turned to me.

"Are we back to drowning him?" Marta asked.

"That YouTube channel we watched," I said. "Remember? At our sleepover?"

"We watched all those music videos," Sophie said. "Weren't we dancing when your cousin started to climb through the window?"

"No," I said. "Not the music videos. We were watching that channel with the teenagers. Remember? They were smashing fruit and then—"

"The Unwatchables," Lissa said. "They are a riot. They do all this wild stuff and make a million dollars from it, and never get in trouble."

"Yes. That's it. The Unwatchables," I said. "Marta, where's your laptop? We have to find an episode."

"You want to smash fruit?" Lissa said.

"Not that one." I climbed to my feet and followed the others to Marta's bedroom.

We huddled around her desk and found the YouTube channel. The Unwatchables had at least a hundred episodes. How could they dream up so many weird projects and sick things to do?

Marta sat on her desk chair and scrolled down the list of episodes.

"Stop right there!" I cried. "There it is. We have to watch that one."

Marta glanced back at me. "'Slime Time'?"

I nodded. "Yes. That's the one. Perfect."

"I remember it," Sophie said. "It was totally gross. They mixed a huge vat of gooey blue slime and poured it over someone."

Lissa poked me. "Is that your idea, Amy? We

make a big batch of blue slime and dump it over Arnie?"

"Well . . . yes," I said. "But—"

"Not good enough," Lissa said. "That's a lame revenge. We need to embarrass him. We need to punish him. We need—"

Marta nodded. "Lissa is right. Blue slime just isn't *bad* enough. If we dump a gallon of slime over his head, Arnie will probably think it's funny."

"You didn't let me finish," I said. "The important thing is *when* we do it to him. We have to embarrass him in front of everyone he knows."

"When is that?" Lissa asked.

"His birthday party," I said. "Next week."

"Where's his party?" Marta asked.

"At Jump Street. You know. The trampoline place for kids," I said. "Arnie invited his whole class. Everyone he knows will be there. We can slime him and totally embarrass him—"

"And ruin his birthday," Lissa said. "Give him something his friends will always remember. They'll probably tease him about it for the rest of his life."

"Yes! Yes!" Marta pounded her desk. "I like it. I *love* it!"

"And what if he turns out to be allergic to it, and it gives him a horrible skin rash?" Sophie added. Did I mention that Sophie is obsessed with allergies and skin rashes?

"That would be an extra bonus," I said. I squeezed Marta's shoulder. "Play the episode. Let's watch how they do it. I think maybe we have the perfect revenge."

So we played the video. Actually, we played it twice. We learned what we needed to make the slime. How to mix it. And the best way to dump it over someone so it stuck to them and slowly oozed into their every pore.

Watching the video, I was excited and eager to get started.

How could I have known it was probably the worst idea of my life?

CHAPTER 22

THE SLIMIEST SLIME

Lissa and I worked down in her basement. Her dad is a carpenter, and he has a big workshop there.

We found an enormous plastic pot in a pile of vases. It held at least three gallons. Lissa said it used to hold a six-foot-tall rubber tree plant, but the plant died.

Perfect for holding our slime.

Making the mixture was harder than I thought it would be. We watched the video three or four more times. But we just couldn't get our slime right.

Ours was too watery. Too thin. We needed the

slime to stick to Arnie and ooze down his body slowly. We wanted him to struggle in front of everyone he knew. We wanted him to choke and fight the slime and try to pull it from his eyes and wipe it from his clothes and slip and fall in it and kick and wallow and cry and . . . and . . .

Lissa and I had big plans for the slime. So it had to be perfect.

But we kept messing up. We kept adding more detergent and flour to thicken it. But each batch we mixed wasn't quite gooey enough.

I dipped my hand into the second batch we made, and the slime just dripped right off my fingers.

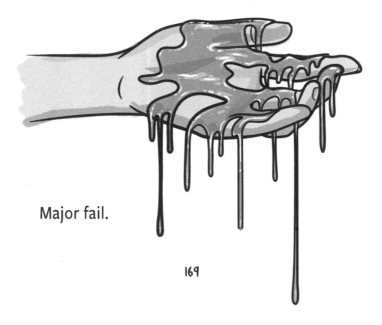

Major fail.

"How can we make it thicker? More gluey?" I said.

Lissa thought for a moment. "Maybe add glue?"

We watched the YouTube video again. The Unwatchables guys used flour to make their slime thick. But Lissa and I had already used two big bags of flour. It made the slime lumpy but not thick enough.

She walked over to her dad's supply cabinet and fumbled around on the shelves. A minute later, she came back gripping a small tube. "This might work."

She held it up so I could read the label.

"Wacky Glue?" I said.

She nodded. "It's supposed to be the stickiest glue on earth. You can stick anything to anything with this."

I took the tube and rolled it around in my hand. "What if it's *too* sticky?" I said.

"This tiny tube? In such a huge pot?" She shook her head. "No way. Listen to me, Amy. This is going to solve the problem."

"Can we test it first?" I asked.

"We've already mixed three batches," she said. "I've got a lot of homework, and so do you. Let's just make the slime, and we can test it when we pour it on Arnie at his party."

That made me laugh. "Awesome idea."

So we made another batch of slime. This batch almost filled the big plastic pot to the top.

When it was nearly done, we squeezed the tube of Wacky Glue into the mixture. Then we stirred it with a small garden spade we'd found under the worktable.

"Definitely thicker," I said. "But not too thick."

"Definitely slimier," Lissa added. "It may be the slimiest slime ever."

"Just what Arnie deserves," I said.

But as it turned out, it wasn't exactly what WE deserved.

CHAPTER 23

PARTY TIME

"This is a big day for Arnie," Mom said as we crossed the parking lot in front of Jump Street. "He doesn't have many friends. So he's totally excited that his whole class will be here."

Arnie and Dad were already inside the building. Dad was probably moving the balloons and decorations around in there. He likes everything to be perfect.

"Hope Arnie doesn't mess it up," I said.

Mom held up both hands with her fingers crossed. "He promised he'd be on his best behavior. He said now that he's nine, he's going to be perfect."

"A perfect *what*?" I said.

Mom gave my hand a gentle slap. "Bad attitude, Amy. Let's give him a chance." She reached over and lifted my bangs. "The word is almost gone. Just a gray blur now."

Two SUVs pulled up to the front door. Kids came bursting out. I saw Arnie's friend Kwame. He waved to us and ran into the building.

"I never told you this," Mom said. "But what your brother did to you was terrible. And I'm so proud of you that you were able to forgive him."

Forgive him? I wanted to burst out laughing.

Mom started to say more. But I saw Lissa's dad's car pull into the parking lot. "There's Lissa," I said. "She's coming to help with the kids."

I gave Mom a little push. "You go on inside. We'll be there in a minute."

I waited till Mom walked through the entrance. Then I hurried to Lissa's car. Her dad helped us lift the big pot of slime from his trunk. We carried it to the side of the building and set it down.

"What are you going to do with that stuff?" he asked.

"It's kind of an arts and crafts project," I told him.

He nodded and started back to the car. "Call me later, Lissa, when you want a ride home."

We watched him drive off.

"We can leave the slime here till it's time for it," I said. "No one will see it over here."

Lissa rubbed her hands together and did her impression of an evil laugh. "Payback day. I'm excited. Are you?"

"I'm pumped," I said. "I dreamed about Arnie swimming in an ocean of slime last night. He was kicking like crazy and splashing and yelling for help. It was an awesome dream."

"Well, let's make the dream come true," Lissa said. She led the way inside.

Jump Street is a popular party place for kids. It's a huge open space, four times bigger than a gym. In one area, the floor is covered with rows of square black trampolines. That's right. The trampolines are in the floor. So the kids can jump as high as they like, and if they fall off, they won't go very far.

The place also has a ball pit filled with colorful

plastic balls. Kids can leap into the pit and sink down and bury themselves in plastic balls and roll around in them and go nuts.

There's also a climbing wall. And some mile-high slides. And a pizza restaurant. And an ice cream bar.

The place was already crowded. Kids were jumping their brains out and diving into the ball pit and running berserk around the building.

Lissa pressed her hands over her ears. "What a racket!" she exclaimed. "Why are little kids so shrill?"

"Maybe because they're kids?" I said.

I searched for Arnie. I finally spotted him shoving kids and knocking them off a trampoline. So much for Mister Perfect.

Dad walked by carrying a big stack of pizza boxes. He had a wide smile on his face. "A big turnout," he said. "Do you believe the energy?"

"Lots of energy," I shouted. "Do you want help?"

He didn't hear me. He walked on.

Arnie came strutting by. He had shopping bags filled with birthday presents in both hands, and he had a candy bar shoved into his mouth.

He's having an awesome time, I thought. *Am I really going to do this? Ruin his party for him? Embarrass him in front of everyone?*

"Great party!" I shouted over the booming crowd voices.

Arnie raised a foot—and stomped as hard as he could on my left shoe.

I let out a cry and hopped back on my right foot. "Owwww. Why'd you do that?"

He spit the candy bar onto my shoe. "I'm the birthday boy," he said. "I can do whatever I want."

Okay, yes. I AM really going to do this, I told myself. *Not a hard decision to make.*

I lifted the wet candy bar off my shoe and went in search of a trash can. Then I found Lissa at the food tables. She was helping my dad unpack the pizza boxes.

She stepped up close to me to make sure he couldn't hear. "Is it showtime?" she asked.

I shook my head. "Let's wait till they bring out

the birthday cake. Maybe we'll sneak up behind him when he goes to blow out the candles."

"Perfect," Lissa said, grinning. "Everyone will be watching."

A sharp *bang* made the room go silent. Some kids screamed.

Another loud explosion.

I gasped and turned toward the sound. More kids cried out in alarm.

—POP! —

I saw Arnie with a fork in his hand. He was running along the balloon decorations, popping them as he ran.

Kids sighed in relief. Lots of kids burst out laughing.

My brother was ruining the decorations that people had worked so hard to put up. Popping the

balloons and laughing his head off.

I saw Mom standing by the ball pit. She had her hands pressed over her cheeks and her eyes shut.

Dad made a move to go after Arnie to stop him. But I saw him

—POP! —

change his mind. He turned away, shaking his head, as the sound of popping balloons rang off the walls.

Arnie finally got tired of destroying the balloons. He tossed the fork away, leaped high, and did a cannonball into the ball pit. He landed hard on his back, send-ing kids scrambling out from under him.

"It's a good thing he promised to be good," Dad said. "Otherwise, I'd be a little upset with him."

I think Dad was making a joke. Lissa and I helped him spread the paper cake plates out on the tables. All I could think about was the big vat of blue slime waiting outside. Why was time moving so slowly?

Finally. Finally.

Mom and Dad called everyone to the tables. Ev-eryone ate their pizza. Now it was birthday cake time.

Arnie perched on his knees on his chair. All his

friends watched as he drummed his plastic fork and knife on the table. His friend Kwame sat beside him, slapping Arnie on the back.

180

Lissa and I stood off to the side. We had carried the heavy pot of slime into the building without being seen. We stood in front of it, blocking it from view.

I could feel my heart start to pound. My hands were suddenly cold.

Yes, I was nervous. Nervous that we might somehow mess up.

I glanced at Lissa. She was blinking and biting her bottom lip. I could see she was as stressed as I was.

Don't blow this, I told myself. *This is your big moment. Your big moment of revenge.*

Two waiters in blue uniforms appeared from the kitchen. They carried the tall chocolate birthday cake on a big tray between them.

I flashed Lissa a thumbs-up. We both turned and raised the slime pot from the bottom. I wanted to do this by myself. But the pot was too heavy. I needed Lissa.

We staggered under its weight. But we forced ourselves to move fast.

The waiters set the cake down on the table in front of Arnie.

Sliding our shoes sideways, we crept up behind him.

The kids all started to sing "Happy Birthday."

Lissa and I moved closer . . . closer.

As soon as the kids stopped singing, Arnie leaned forward to blow out the candles.

Lissa and I stepped up behind him.

We raised the pot high. Turned it upside down.

And watched the blue slime plop over his head.

CHAPTER 24

A WONDERFUL MOMENT

The heavy glob of slime made a loud *swwwaaaaassssh* sound as it crashed over Arnie's head. Kind of like a high ocean wave smashing into rocks.

Lissa and I froze, holding the pot between us. And we watched the thick goo ooze over my brother's head and slide down over his shoulders. So slowly, as if we were watching it in slow motion.

Mom and Dad were standing across the table from Arnie. Only their eyes moved. They grew wider until I thought they might pop out of their heads.

The kids all stayed silent for the longest time. Mouths dropped open but no sound came out.

I heard a *clannnng* and saw the two waiters drop the empty cake tray on the floor.

Finally, screams rose up. Shrill cries of surprise. Chairs scraped as kids jumped to their feet. The screams quickly turned to laughter.

Arnie had been leaning forward to blow out the candles on the cake. I watched him trying to straighten up under the thick blanket of slime. Now the blue goo covered his shoulders entirely and was sliding slowly down over his shirt.

Arnie thrashed his hands, and his whole body squirmed as he tried to free his arms from the gunk. He tugged at the slime that covered his face. He frantically pulled at it with both hands.

When Mom and Dad saw that he was struggling to breathe, they moved in. They rushed up behind him and tried to help.

Lissa and I lowered the empty pot to the floor and backed away.

"Success!" she whispered. She tried to slap me

a high five, but I was frozen, watching Arnie battling the oozing slime.

Enjoying it too much to move.

I was enjoying it so much I forgot to take photos. Finally, I remembered. I pulled out my phone and took a dozen shots of Arnie squirming under the blue gunk.

"Why? Why?" I turned and saw Mom shouting at me with her hands cupped around her mouth. "Why, Amy? Why?"

What could I say?

She and Dad struggled along with Arnie to free him from the heavy slime blanket.

A wonderful moment.

But only a moment.

In the next second, everything changed.

CHAPTER 25

SLIME DOESN'T PAY

Arnie's chair scraped loudly against the floor as he stood up. The chair fell over and bounced and clattered behind him.

Kids had been shouting and laughing. But the crash of the chair made them go silent.

All eyes were on Arnie as he raised both hands high over his head and let out a long, angry howl.

Mom and Dad leaped back, their eyes wide with alarm.

Arnie stood tall and began to make a grunting noise. He tore patches of slime off his head with both hands.

And then I gasped as I saw him begin to change.

His hands appeared to grow larger, as if they were being inflated. His head rose higher. It took me a while to realize he was growing. His body was stretching... stretching quickly.

His grunts grew louder until they became vicious animal growls.

I grabbed Lissa's hand and we both gaped in horror as dark fur sprouted on his hands ... his arms ... his face!

The shape of his head narrowed. His nose stretched out until it became a long animal snout.

Kids screamed and leaped to their feet. They backed away from the table, arms out as if to protect themselves, eyes wide with terror.

"He—he's a MONSTER!" Lissa cried. "A real monster!"

She grabbed my hand and we held on to each other.

This isn't happening, I thought. *This CAN'T be happening!*

He was NOT one of the monsters I had seen. He was a different monster.

A totally different monster.

Arnie shook his fur-covered body. Patches of blue slime flew off him. He slapped his chest and tore more slime away with his big furry paws.

The two waiters talked rapidly into their phones. Probably calling for help.

Mom and Dad had their arms around each other. Backed against the wall, they stared in open-mouthed horror.

I saw kids running out the front door. Frightened screams and cries rang over the huge room.

I wanted to scream, too. But I held on to Lissa, frozen in terror.

My brother . . . my brother is a MONSTER.

What have I done? What have I DONE?
I did this to him!

On the table in front of Arnie, the candles on the birthday cake were still flickering. He let out a roar and smashed the cake with both paws.

Snapping his jaws, he gazed around the room. His glance stopped on me.

He stared for a long moment, dark eyes glowing. Not moving. Not blinking. Locked on me.

Then he tossed back his monster head and let out a long, angry snarl. I could see his jagged yellow teeth poking out from the bottom of the snout.

He leaped onto the table, his back legs landing hard. Then he dove for me, front paws outstretched.

"Noooo—!"

My scream was cut off as he wrapped his furry arms around my waist. And, grunting and snapping his jaws furiously, he tackled me to the floor.

CHAPTER 26

HOW CAN WE GET ARNIE BACK?

"Get off me!" I screamed. "Get away!"

He pressed his hot face against mine. When I saw his eyes up close, I knew my screams wouldn't help. They weren't Arnie's eyes. They were bloodred monster eyes.

Grunting, snarling, he swiped at me with his heavy paws and snapped his yellow teeth, nipping at my arms, my throat.

I raised both hands and tried to shove him off me. But he was too heavy and too strong.

"Help! Someone help Amy!" I heard Lissa cry.

I saw her dive forward and bend over the monster. She reached for its back to pull it off me. Mom and Dad were close behind her.

But the monster heaved an elbow into Lissa. It sent her tumbling away. She fell with a sharp cry.

I shoved him again. The big creature slapped my hands away. Then it sank its teeth into my wrist.

"Arnie? Can you hear me? Arnie—stop!"

My cries seemed to enrage him. Red eyes glowing, he grabbed my head in both paws. He raised it off the floor—and slammed it back down.

I felt an explosion of pain. Then everything went black.

When I opened my eyes, I didn't know where I was.

A bright ceiling light forced me to close them again. Then I opened them just a slit and tried to raise myself. But a thudding pain at the back of my head made me drop back down.

I blinked a few times. Mom's face appeared above me. Then Dad's. Both of them squinted down at me as if I was some kind of specimen.

"Where . . . am . . . I?" My voice sounded as if it was coming through a thick fog.

"You're home," Mom said. "We brought you home."

"Yes . . . yes, I remember now," I choked out.

"Dr. Wentz was here," Mom said. "You fell asleep after he left. He said you'll be okay. But he told us to watch out for a concussion."

"You hit your head hard," Dad said. "We . . . we were so worried."

I groaned. It was all coming back to me. "How long have I been asleep?"

"Only about twenty minutes," Mom said.

I tried to sit up again. This time I made it.

I glanced around. I was on the living room couch.

"Lissa?" I said. I glanced around the room.

"She's in the bathroom," Mom said. "How do you feel? Are you in pain?"

I touched the back of my head. It ached a little. Nothing terrible.

I blinked a few more times. The room came into sharper focus. "I think I'm okay," I said.

Dad handed me a tall glass of water, and I drank it down. "Amy, why did you do it?" he said.

"Do it?"

"Why did you and Lissa pour that stuff on Arnie?" he asked.

"He deserved it," I said. "He'd been asking for it. We had no choice. Seriously."

Mom reached out and smoothed the side of my hair. "No choice? Do you mean that? Are you thinking clearly? Maybe you *do* have a concussion."

"It was payback, Mom. Arnie was ruining my life. You know that. So Lissa and I came up with the slime plan and—"

"You didn't want to hurt him. You just wanted to embarrass him, right?" Dad said.

I nodded. "Yes. We wanted to embarrass him in front of everyone. But we didn't want to change him into a monster. I mean, who would think—"

I stopped. My eyes darted around the room again. "Hey—where *is* Arnie?"

"Don't you hear him growling?" Dad said. "I locked him in the garage. I didn't know what else to do with him."

"We can't leave him there," Mom said. "The neighbors will call the police."

I swallowed. "Is he still . . ."

"Yes, he's still a monster," Dad said. "Listen. You can hear him trying to bang the garage down."

I listened. I could hear him out there.

I shivered. "This is impossible. IMPOSSIBLE! Kids don't change into monsters. That only happens in horror movies."

Mom sighed. "This is a horror movie, Amy. How are we going to change him back into Arnie?"

They both stared at me.

"Are you expecting me to have an answer?" I said.

Mom dropped down beside me on the couch. "Well . . . you mixed that slime. What did you put in it?"

I shut my eyes. I tried to remember. "We got the recipe on YouTube," I said. "There wasn't anything strange in it. Nothing that could turn a person into a monster."

Mom grabbed my hand. "Tell us what the ingredients were."

"Mostly detergent and flour," a voice said.

I turned and saw Lissa walk into the room. She stepped up behind the couch. "Amy, are you okay?"

I shrugged. "I think so. My head hurts a little."

"I hear those noises out back," Lissa said. "Does that mean Arnie is still a monster? It didn't wear off?"

Mom lowered her eyes. "It didn't wear off," she said.

"Oh no. Oh no." Lissa slapped the sides of her face. "How could this happen? It's like a nightmare!"

I stood up. "Wait a minute. Did you say Dr. Wentz was here? Did you have him look at Arnie?"

"Of course not," Dad replied. "He would have been terrified. Besides, he's not an *animal* doctor!"

"Never mind that," Mom said. "Finish telling me what was in that blue slime."

"Like I said," Lissa replied, "nothing too weird. Water . . . detergent . . . flour . . . blue food coloring . . . We stirred in a couple of raw eggs . . ."

"Oh. And we added a tube of Wacky Glue at the end," I said. "You know. To make it stickier."

Mom shook her head sadly. "Harmless ingredients."

"Except they weren't harmless," Dad said.

A roar from the garage made us all jump.

"What are we going to do?" Mom cried.

"Hold on," I said. "I think I have an idea."

CHAPTER 27

GARAGE SURPRISE

Dad drove us to the Pick n Pay to buy supplies. Then we had to stop at the hardware store to get another tube of Wacky Glue. He dropped us off at Lissa's house, and we carried everything into the basement.

"I seriously hope this works," Lissa said, spreading everything out on her dad's worktable.

"It was the only thing I could think of," I told her. "Mom and Dad seem so puzzled. They don't have any ideas. They're in a total panic. I had to come up with *something*."

"But . . . what are the chances?" Lissa said. "What

are the chances that Arnie will turn back into himself if we dump another load of slime on him? A million to one?"

I sighed. "What are the chances he'd turn into a monster in the first place?"

I searched the basement for another big pot. But I couldn't find one. I picked up a large metal bucket from behind a pile of fertilizer bags. "Let's just use this," I said.

Lissa pulled out her phone. "I think we should check out the Unwatchables video again. Just to make sure we get the mixture right."

She started to punch up the YouTube app. She stopped when her mom called from the top of the basement stairs. "Lissa? Are you home?"

"Yes, I'm down here, Mom," she shouted back. "Amy is with me. We're working on something."

"How was the birthday party?" her mom asked.

"Uh . . . it was interesting," Lissa replied.

"Did you have a good time?"

"Not really," Lissa answered.

I don't think her mom heard her. She just said, "See you later," and went away.

Lissa and I watched the YouTube video. I checked off every ingredient they used. We had the same stuff ready for our mixture. The only difference was the Wacky Glue.

"We need the glue," Lissa said. "We need our new slime to be exactly the same as the first batch."

That made sense. "No problem," I said. "We bought the glue."

She ran up to the kitchen to get a couple of eggs. I filled the bucket two-thirds full of water. Then I dropped in twenty detergent pods, just like the first batch.

Lissa cracked the eggs on the side of the bucket and let the yolks ooze into the mixture. I added a bag of flour. Then she poured in an entire bottle of blue food coloring.

We found a long-handled wooden spoon and took turns stirring the slime. It was nice and thick, just as gooey as the first batch.

When we got it to where it felt right, Lissa squeezed in the tube of Wacky Glue. And we stirred some more.

I called my dad. "The slime is ready. Is Arnie still roaring in the garage?"

"Yes. He's making a deafening racket. We have to hurry. Mrs. Neruda next door has already complained about the noise."

"What did you tell her?"

"I said Arnie was practicing for a rock band."

"Come pick us up," I said. "The bucket is too heavy to carry."

"On my way," he said. "I . . . I sure hope this works."

"Me too," I replied.

What will we do if it doesn't work? What can we try next?

Those questions gave me the shudders.

Lissa held the slime bucket in the back seat, and Dad drove us home. He looked terrible. His eyes were red, his hair unbrushed. His hands were trembling on the steering wheel, and one of his eyes had started to twitch.

"We need a plan," he said. "We can't just walk into the garage and dump it on him. He won't stand still. He'll fight."

I thought about it for a long moment. "What if you and Mom go into the garage first?" I said. "You pretend you're trying to reason with him. You know. Nice and calm."

Dad nearly drove through a stop sign. "Then what?"

"Then you grab him and pin his arms behind his back. When you've got him standing still, Lissa and I will run in and pour the slime over his head."

Dad didn't answer. I could see he was thinking hard.

"Okay," he said finally. "That might work. I . . . I can't think of anything better."

He pulled the car up the driveway and parked at the side of the house. I helped Lissa carry the heavy bucket out of the car. A little blue goo splashed onto the driveway. I held the bucket in both hands, trying to steady it.

Dad ran into the house through the front door. A few minutes later, he came running out with Mom. She looked frazzled, too, and her coat was buttoned wrong.

She didn't greet us. She stared at the slime bucket and said, "Let's hurry." She raised both hands. She had her fingers crossed.

She and Dad led the way along the side of the house toward the garage. Lissa and I followed, both of us with a hand on the bucket handle, trying not to spill any more.

We were nearly to the garage when Dad opened his mouth in a cry. He and Mom stopped short.

"Oh!" Lissa and I almost bumped them from behind.

"What's wrong?" I said. And then I answered my own question.

The side of the garage was shattered. The shingles were scattered over the grass. Cracked, broken boards formed a jagged hole in the wall.

Arnie was gone.

CHAPTER 28

SLIME DOESN'T PAY AGAIN

The bucket fell from our hands and thudded onto the ground. The four of us stood there with our mouths hanging open.

"Where is he?" Dad cried, gazing all around. "Where did he go?"

We didn't have to wait long for an answer.

We heard a roar from somewhere down the block. And then a woman's shrill scream.

Dad spun to the street. "We have to catch him. If anyone gets hurt . . ."

He grabbed the bucket by the handle, raised it to

his side, and started to run. Mom, Lissa, and I went racing after him.

Another roar. Another scream.

I heard the squeal of car brakes. A shattering crash.

More screams. Car horns blasted.

Blue slime sloshed over the sides of the bucket as Dad ran with it.

Lissa and I raced at full speed to keep up with him. Mom fell back, holding her side. She doesn't run very much.

Arnie, the monster, came into view at the end of the block. A crowd had gathered to watch him smashing the windows of an SUV with his powerful, fur-covered fists. He let out a sharp roar with each punch. People ducked as shards of glass flew everywhere.

Two women had their phones raised. They were recording the frightening scene. I saw others speaking excitedly into their phones. Two little kids were hiding behind their parents, crying loudly. Over their cries, I heard the high wail of sirens in the far distance.

"Arnie—!" Dad screamed. "Stop! STOP! Do you hear me?"

The monster snarled in reply, showing his curled yellow teeth. He waved his claws at Dad, motioning him to stay back.

But Dad crept closer. He raised the slime bucket slowly in front of him.

"Arnie—come away from there," Dad shouted. "Time to come home."

The crowd had grown silent. Phones were raised. No one spoke. No one moved.

The monster pulled his lips back and bared his teeth again. Then he spun around and swung his fist into the SUV windshield.

People screamed as the glass cracked.

The monster swung again. Shattering it. Snarling, he punched the remaining pieces into the front of the car.

Dad moved closer. I could see his arm tense. He was getting ready to pour the slime over Arnie.

I stood trembling beside Dad. Lissa grabbed my shoulder. She was breathing hard, gaping wide eyed at the Arnie monster.

Suddenly, the monster sprang away from the car. He dove forward, lowered his head—and grabbed me.

The monster wrapped his powerful arms around my waist.

"Noooo!" I screamed as I felt myself lifted off the ground.

"Arnie! It's me! I'm your sister! Arnie—NO!"

I tried to twist free. But the monster's arms tightened around my waist. And lifted me ... lifted me ...

... just as Dad swung the bucket high and sent the slime rushing out.

No time to scream or cry out. The monster held me up in front of him as the slime flew out of the bucket.

I shut my eyes as the thick blue gunk washed over me. It oozed slowly over my head, over my eyes, into my nose. I started to choke. I couldn't breathe.

The slime oozed over my shoulders . . . covered my arms . . . Thick and heavy, it slid down my whole body.

The monster. Completely dry. Used me as his shield.

Then he tossed me away. And I dropped to my knees on the pavement as the cold blue slime clung to me.

And my only thought as I shivered beneath the blanket of slime: *Am I going to change into a monster now?*

CHAPTER 29

A FRIEND TO THE RESCUE

Shivering under the heavy blanket of slime, I felt someone grab me by the elbows and pull me to my feet. Dad.

He held me up. Then someone was wiping the goo from my eyes. Mom had taken off her coat and was wiping my face with it, my hair . . . trying to rub the gluey slime off my arms.

"Hurry! Arnie ran off." Dad pointed. "I think he's heading into town."

I rubbed more slime away from my eyes. I could see people scattering in all directions. Some were hurrying back to their houses. Others were chasing after the monster. The parents pulled the two crying kids away.

The sirens still sounded in the distance.

"We have to go after him," Dad said, his voice shaking. "He's going to do more damage. And . . . he might hurt someone."

"We'll catch him," I said.

But how?

I suddenly had an idea. I pulled Lissa close. "Listen to me," I whispered. "You can be a hero. I just thought of something that might help us."

She listened carefully to my idea. Then she nodded her head solemnly. "Worth a try," she said and took off running.

Dad bumped my shoulder. "Did you hear that crash? He's smashing something else." He tugged my hand. "Let's go!"

The three of us started to run down the middle of the street.

Slime splashed off me as we ran. I moved close to Mom. "Am I changing?"

She blinked at me.

"Are you *what*?"

"Am I changing into a monster?"

She shook her head.
"No. You're not changing.
Of course not."

Of course not?

What does that mean?

I heard screams up ahead.

Again the shrill sound of shattering glass.

And there he was, on Prince Street. Swinging high on a lamppost. He had climbed it, and he was smashing the light with his big fist.

With a roar, the monster leaped down from the top of the lamppost. He landed with a hard *thud* on all fours. Then he stood upright and gazed around.

Looking for more damage he could do?

"Arnie—it's me—your sister!" I cried.

His red eyes locked on mine. Grunting, he took a few lumbering steps toward me.

Mom pulled me away. "Amy—get back. He'll just attack you again."

I stumbled a few steps away from him. And then I saw someone. Someone I recognized.

Kwame. Stepping out of his house across the street. Heading for Arnie.

"Kwame! Get back! Stay away! It isn't safe!" I screamed.

He trotted over to me and gazed at the monster. "Amy—Arnie . . . Why did this happen to him? Can he change back?"

"I don't know. But don't get any closer," I warned. "He . . . he's dangerous."

"Maybe he'll listen to me, Amy," Kwame said. "Maybe I can calm him down."

He started toward the monster, but I grabbed him.

"No. Don't try, Kwame. It isn't safe."

"But I'm his best friend. He always listens to me."

"I'm his sister," I replied. "He tried to *hurt* me!"

A thin smile crossed Kwame's lips. "But he likes me better than you," he said. He pushed past me. "Let me give it a try."

He took a deep breath and began to stride toward the monster.

CHAPTER 30

KWAME IN DANGER

Kwame cupped his hands around his mouth and shouted, "Arnie—I'm here. Arnie—it's me!"

A new group of people had gathered. But they grew silent as Kwame stepped nearer the monster.

"Arnie? Do you want to talk?" Kwame called. "Do you want to talk to me?"

The monster turned and narrowed his eyes at Kwame. Drool oozed from his open mouth. He curled his furry paws into fists and lowered them to his sides.

"It's me," Kwame said, tapping his chest. "You recognize me, right?"

The monster grunted a reply. He rubbed the side of his face with a furry paw and moved his jaw up and down.

Kwame took another step forward.

I watched, frozen in fear. I didn't move. I didn't breathe.

Would Kwame calm Arnie enough so we could take him home?

We didn't have to wait long for an answer.

With an angry roar, the monster dove forward. He grabbed Kwame by the neck—and lifted him off the ground.

Kwame made a startled *ulllllp* sound. He thrashed both arms in the air and kicked with his legs.

But the monster held on tight. He kept one big paw wrapped around Kwame's neck. He carried him to another lamppost and began to climb it with his free paw.

People screamed. Some turned away.

"Put him down!" I heard my dad shout.

And then the whole crowd was shouting it. "Put him down! Put him down! Put him down!"

The monster climbed nearly to the top. Kwame had gone still, afraid to make any kind of move.

Dad gripped my shoulder. "What is he going to do? Is he going to toss Kwame? Is he going to drop him?" He held onto me as if he needed me to hold him up.

We both gazed up as the monster carried Kwame by the neck to the top of the lamppost.

"He—he's going to drop him!" I stammered to Dad. "He's up so high. He's going to—" I couldn't finish my sentence. I started to choke.

The monster dangled him high over us. Shook him. Prepared to drop him.

I turned when I heard a shout from behind me.

"Wait! Wait!"

I turned and saw Lissa running toward us at full speed.

I saw what she was carrying.

Would she be in time to save Kwame? Would my idea work?

CHAPTER 31

TEMPTING THE MONSTER

"Out of the way! Out of the way!"

Lissa elbowed her way through the crowd. Most people didn't even notice her. They had their eyes on Kwame and the monster high above.

I stepped up to her. I took the tall paper cup from her hand. "Thanks. Fingers crossed," I said.

I turned and raced to the lamppost. I raised the paper cup over my head. "Arnie—this is for you!" I shouted.

I held the cup high and waved it. "Arnie, it's your favorite!" I screamed. "Lissa brought you your favorite!"

I held it higher. "An orange smoothie!" I cried.
"Lissa brought you a smoothie."

People in the crowd started to murmur and buzz.
Of course, they didn't have a clue about what I was
trying to do.

The monster dangled Kwame high over the sidewalk. Finally, he lowered his head and stared down at the drink.

My teeth were clenched so hard my jaw ached. This was too horrifying to bear. I felt I might explode into a million pieces as I waved the cup at him.

The crowd grew silent. Kwame had been screaming his head off. But now he grew silent, too. His arms went limp at his sides.

The monster stared at the cup . . . Stared . . .

"He . . . he's going to DROP me!" Kwame screamed.

People gasped. Some cried out in horror.

My heart felt like it had jumped into my throat. I couldn't move. I couldn't blink. And as I stared up at the monster, I saw his paw loosen on the lamppost.

I gasped as he started to slide down. Gripping Kwame by the neck, he slid slowly . . . slowly . . . down, releasing Kwame when his feet hit the ground.

Kwame let out a happy cry as his shoes touched the grass. He tossed his hands in the air and pumped both fists above his head. Then he went racing away, screaming happily.

He didn't look back. A few seconds later, he disappeared into his house.

Some people cheered. Others backed away as the monster lurched forward. He swung his furry arm and swiped the cup from my hand. He grabbed it so hard I tumbled backward.

The monster raised the cup to his open mouth and poured the orange drink down his throat in one big gulp. He licked his lips with a fat tongue and heaved the cup into the street.

His burp sounded like a bass drum exploding.

Then he turned and stared at Lissa. Stared hard at her, dark eyes glowing, fur-covered arms at his sides.

Now what? I thought.

Now what?

CHAPTER 32

THE TRUTH ABOUT ARNIE

To my surprise, the big creature's shoulders slumped. He opened his mouth with a sigh. He lowered his head. The air seemed to go out of him.

"Arnie—?" I cried. "That smoothie. Did it help you?"

I gasped as he moved forward and reached for me. He gently wrapped his paw around my hand. He started to lead me away from the crowd.

Holding my hand, he led me to Mom and Dad. He put his arms around them, lowered his eyes to the ground, shaking his head as if apologizing.

Lissa followed us across the grass. "It worked!" she cried. "The orange smoothie—it tamed him, just like at the mall."

I slapped her a high five. Then I hugged her. "Lissa, you're a hero!"

We started to walk toward home.

"We have to buy more orange smoothies to make sure he stays calm," Dad said. "I'll go right away. I'll buy a gallon. I'll buy *two* gallons!"

"But we can't just keep feeding smoothies to a monster," Mom said. "There's got to be a way . . ." Her voice trailed off.

I had an idea.

"One orange smoothie made him calm," I said. "Maybe a *second* smoothie will turn him back into Arnie."

The monster rubbed his paws together hungrily and made slurping noises with his tongue.

"It's worth a try," Dad said.

We walked up the driveway.

"What should we do with him?" Mom asked. "I don't feel safe letting him walk around in the house. Who knows how long the smoothie will keep him quiet."

"Well, we can't put him in the garage," Dad said. "He broke the garage wide open."

"Wish we had a basement," I said.

"Why not just lock him in his room?" Lissa said. She patted him on the shoulder. "You'll be a good boy, won't you, Arnie? You'll wait for your smoothie?"

The monster nodded and made more slurping noises.

So that's what we did. We locked him in his room.

Then, Mom, Lissa, and I waited tensely in the kitchen for Dad to return with the orange smoothies. Mom chewed her bottom lip and tapped her fingers on the tabletop. Lissa and I didn't talk. We were full-time waiting.

Dad finally arrived home with six tall cups of orange smoothies. We followed close behind him as he carried a cup to Arnie's room.

Mom unlocked the door. The monster pulled it open.

Dad reached the smoothie cup out to him. "Here you go. Hope this works."

The monster yanked the cup from Dad's hand. He raised it high and poured the smoothie down his throat. It made a *glug glug glug* sound as he swallowed it.

Another loud burp shook the walls.

The four of us stood in the safety of the hall. We watched the monster through the open door. Watched . . . Watched without saying a word.

Please work. Please turn Arnie back into Arnie, I silently begged.

We stood there in the hall, gazing at the monster. I kept crossing and uncrossing my arms. Tensely shoving my hands into my pockets, then out again.

We watched him for five minutes . . . ten minutes . . . It seemed like hours.

Nothing happened. Nothing. He didn't change. He stood there breathing hard, orange smoothie staining his lips.

Finally, Dad let out a long sigh. "Failure," he murmured.

He took the door key from Mom, closed the bedroom door, and locked the monster in.

Mom shook her head sadly. "Come with me," she said, her voice just above a whisper. "It's time. Time for me to tell you the truth about Arnie."

CHAPTER 33

THE HAPPY ENDING

Lissa and I followed her into the living room. We sat down on the couch. Mom and Dad took armchairs across the coffee table from us.

Mom swallowed a few times, then cleared her throat. She clasped her hands tightly in her lap. "This is hard to say," she started. She cleared her throat again.

"Amy, I knew that someday I'd have to tell you the truth about your brother."

My hands were suddenly cold. I tucked them into my jeans pockets. "The truth?" I said.

She nodded. "What happened to Arnie was not

your fault. The slime you poured on him did not turn Arnie into a monster."

"Huh?" Lissa and I both gasped.

"But, Mom—" I started.

She held up a hand to silence me.

"You didn't turn Arnie into a monster," she said, "because *he always was a monster.*"

"That's the truth," Dad chimed in. "Arnie was born a monster. We knew he was a monster when we adopted him."

"That's one of the reasons we adopted him," Mom added, her voice just above a whisper. "No one wanted him. We felt so bad for him."

I stared from one of them to the other. Was this some kind of joke?

No. They were dead serious.

"The blue slime you made brought out the *real* Arnie," Mom said.

"But—but—" I sputtered.

"Didn't you wonder why your brother was always so horrible to everyone?" Dad asked. "Didn't you wonder why he was such a bad baby and such a bad kid? Absolutely the worst brother anyone could have?"

"We couldn't do anything to make him behave better," Mom said. "We knew we couldn't control him because we knew he was a monster."

"But we thought maybe living with a family would change him," Dad said. "That's what we hoped for."

Lissa and I stared across the table at my parents. Their words were spinning in my mind. I struggled to make sense of what they were saying.

"But . . . he was such a cute baby," I said.

"He was cute," Mom said. "But don't you remember? He liked to bite people? Whenever I tried to take his picture or pick him up from his crib, he tried to bite my hand."

"Amy, we haven't been completely honest with you. I want to apologize," Dad said. "We tried to keep the truth from you. And that was a mistake."

I gasped. "Huh? Am I a monster, too?"

They smiled and shook their heads. "No. Not at all," Mom said.

"But the other monsters..." Dad said. "The one in your room with the quills... and the one that chased you to Sophie's house ... they were both Arnie."

"Huh?" I gasped. "I ... don't understand."

"From time to time, when he was very little, Arnie's true self would come out," Dad continued. "He'd become a monster for a short while. And each time, he was a *different* monster."

Mom sighed. "So strange. He never looked the same twice." She shook her head. "I don't think he could control it."

"But he hasn't done that in years. And he could always turn himself back to Arnie after a few minutes," Dad said. "Before today, he never stayed a monster for long. It was easy to keep the secret about him."

"But today, the blue slime did something to him," Mom said. "The slime got in his pores. It's keeping him from changing back to Arnie. He—he's a monster to stay now."

Her voice broke. She wiped away a tear from one eye.

"But, Mom . . ." I started. "Why did you let us think a second dose of slime would turn him back?"

Mom sniffed and gave me a watery, half-hearted smile. "You wanted to help so much. And we really just weren't ready to tell you. I'm sorry."

"Well . . . what are we going to do with him?" I asked. "We can't keep him in his room forever."

"And you can't just keep giving him orange smoothies to keep him calm," Lissa said.

Dad shook his head. "I don't know," he murmured. "I don't know what to do."

Mom let out a sigh. She cradled her head in her hands. "I wish I knew . . ." she said in a whisper.

Dad's phone rang.

He pulled it from his pocket and squinted at the screen. Then he jumped up, raised it to his ear, and took the call in the kitchen.

Lissa, Mom, and I sat staring at one another. No one spoke. My head was spinning.

I could hear Arnie the monster banging around in his room down the hall.

After a few minutes, Dad strode back into the

living room. To my surprise, he had a big smile on his face. He waved his phone in front of him.

"Who was that?" Mom asked.

"You won't believe this," Dad said. He dropped back onto his chair. "You remember Stephen Craven? The guy I worked for a few years ago. The director who does all those horror films?"

"Yes," Mom replied. "Of course I remember him."

"Well, that was Craven." Dad nodded, still grinning.

"What did he want?" I asked.

"He saw Arnie on the news," Dad said. "He saw him smashing cars and climbing light poles and terrifying people. Craven said the videos are all over the internet."

"Yes?" Mom said. "And?"

"Craven thinks Arnie is an awesome-looking monster," Dad said. "He saw us leading Arnie away and he recognized me. That's why he called. He wants Arnie to star in his new movie—*Slime Doesn't Pay*."

"Huh?" Mom's eyes bulged, and she jumped to her feet.

Lissa and I exchanged amazed glances.

"Craven called Arnie the SlimeBeast," Dad said. "He thinks he could do a whole series of SlimeBeast movies and make millions of dollars."

"Yaaaaay!" Mom let out an excited cry. She and Dad hugged. Lissa and I slapped high fives.

"We're saved!" Mom cried. "No more money problems. We're saved!"

Dad turned to me. "Amy, go let Arnie out of his room. He's going to be a *star*!"

AFTERWORD

So, okay. Now you know the whole story.

Yes, I told you. I did something *horrible* to my brother.

But it paid off big-time.

And now I'm a revenge expert.

Listen. Do you have a horrible little brother or sister?

I can help you. I can help you plan your perfect revenge.

Slime? No. Let's stay away from slime.

Been there, done that.

I saw something new on The Unwatchables.

We just need some shaving cream and gummy worms.

It could be awesome!

Come on. Let's give it a try.

THE END

R. L. STINE

has more than 400 million English-language books in print, plus international editions in thirty-two languages, making him one of the most popular children's authors of all time. Besides Goosebumps, he has written series including Fear Street, Rotten School, Mostly Ghostly, the Nightmare Room, Dangerous Girls, and Just Beyond. Stine lives in New York City with his wife, Jane, an editor and publisher.